SCHOOL OF FEAR

SCHOOL OF FEAR
THE FINAL EXAM

BY
GITTY DANESHVARI

ILLUSTRATED BY
CARRIE GIFFORD

LITTLE, BROWN AND COMPANY
New York • Boston

Little, Brown and Company
Hachette Book Group
237 Park Avenue, New York, NY 10017
Visit our website at www.lb-kids.com

Little, Brown and Company is a division of Hachette Book Group, Inc.
The Little, Brown name and logo are trademarks of Hachette Book Group, Inc.

The publisher is not responsible for websites (or their content) that
are not owned by the publisher.

First Edition: October 2011

Library of Congress Cataloging-in-Publication Data

Daneshvari, Gitty.
The final exam / written by Gitty Daneshvari ; illustrated by Carrie Gifford. —
1st ed.   p. cm. — (School of Fear ; 3)
Summary: When a reporter plans an exposé that could shut down the School
of Fear, Garrison, Lulu, Madeleine, Theo, and Hyacinth seek help from Bishop
Basmati, head of the nearby Contrary Conservatory, whose hyperactive, fearless,
and extremely impulsive students soon overrun the School of Fearians.
ISBN 978-0-316-18287-4
[1. Phobias — Fiction.   2. Schools — Fiction.   3. Interpersonal relations — Fiction.
4. Self-actualization (Psychology) — Fiction.   5. Reporters and reporting —
Fiction.   6. Tabloid newspapers — Fiction.   7. Massachusetts — Fiction.]
I. Gifford, Carrie, ill. II. Title.
PZ7.D2073Fin 2011   [Fic] — dc23   2011012964

10 9 8 7 6 5 4 3 2
RRD-C
Printed in the United States of America

In memory of

Omar Chaudhery

SCHOOL OF FEAR

SCHOOL OF FEAR

The wilderness outside Farmington, Massachusetts
(Exact location withheld for security purposes)
Direct all correspondence to PO Box 333, Farmington, MA 01201

Dear Parental Units,

I write to you today with terrible news, perhaps the worst news ever! Don't worry—your children are still alive and well. Or perhaps that is a bit of an overstatement; they are definitely still *alive.*

In an unforeseen turn of events, School of Fear finds itself on the brink of total and utter ruin. Rather regrettably, one of our students (I'm not mentioning any names, but she does have a certain fondness for ferrets) informed tabloid reporter Sylvie Montgomery not only of our existence, but of our deepest secret! And now, with a mere three weeks to stop the publication of the career-annihilating article, your children have chosen to stay on and fight.

So while you may see them simply as your children or, as I once did, as an arachnophobe (Madeleine), a thanatophobe (Theo), an aquaphobe (Garrison), a claustrophobe (Lulu), and an isolophobe (Hyacinth), I assure you they are much more. Regardless of the outcome, they shall return to you different than they came to me a year ago, or even at the start of this very summer, and that is because they *are* different. They are School of Fearians.

With smudged mascara and a heavy heart, but still very attractive,

Mrs. Wellington

MRS. WELLINGTON

CHAPTER 1

EVERYONE'S AFRAID OF SOMETHING:

Autodysomophobia is the fear

of emitting a vile odor.

The end is not the end. And that is certainly not to imply that the end is actually the beginning or the middle, for that would be most inaccurate. The end is simply far more than a completion point or finish line. The end is a call for courage, rallying those ready for the next journey.

Thirteen-year-old Madeleine Masterson was sound asleep, with her raven locks tucked neatly beneath a shower cap and her serene blue eyes sealed tightly to the world. Only a year earlier, Madeleine had arrived at School of Fear adorned in a netted veil and a belt of repellents, desperate to keep all spiders and creepy crawlers at bay. While the politically savvy London native had shed both the belt and veil after her first summer, there had been quite a relapse as of late. A few days earlier Madeleine had come to blows with a brown and burgundy Balinese spider, culminating in arachnid road-kill on her forehead. The traumatic incident immediately sparked a renewed sense of panic, hence the implementation of the shower cap.

On this particular morning, it was not her usual hallucination of eight sticky feet dancing across her arm that awoke her, but something far more harmless. With her eyes still tightly sealed, Madeleine noticed a pungent scent. It wasn't that of smoke or any recognizable danger. Thick and musty, the overwhelmingly saccharine odor lingered in both her mouth and nostrils. While Madeleine had always enjoyed the odd sweet, there was something downright nauseating about this smell. Now, if this had been any other day, she would have instantly opened her eyes and satiated her curiosity. But on this particular morning Madeleine could think of nothing quite as frightening as facing the hours ahead.

"Madeleine," a familiar voice whispered, warm billows of breath cascading against the young girl's cheeks.

Having no recourse, Madeleine relented and slowly unlocked her eyes. A mere inch from her face was School of Fear's eccentric headmistress, Mrs. Wellington. And while some people may look good up close, she certainly was not one of them. Thick layers of makeup sat unflatteringly atop the old woman's deep and jagged wrinkles, showing her skin to be a most merciless record of time past.

"Good morning, Mrs. Wellington," Madeleine whispered awkwardly before once again finding her olfactory gland overwhelmed by the stench. "Not to be cheeky, but what on earth is that smell?"

"I've never cared much for body odor, so I had Schmidty replace my eccrine glands with marmalade and honey. Lovely, isn't it?"

"But Schmidty isn't a doctor!" Madeleine exclaimed.

"No, but he pretended to be one quite frequently as a child."

"That hardly matters."

"Shush," Mrs. Wellington replied. "You'll wake the others. We haven't time for idle chitchat; you must meet me in the classroom at once."

Madeleine looked into the old woman's face and nodded. There was an understandable urgency in the air as Mrs. Wellington prepared to face her two greatest fears: Abernathy, and losing the school. Far more than an estranged stepson, Abernathy was Mrs. Wellington's lone failure as a teacher—a truth she could barely admit to herself, let alone to the world.

As Mrs. Wellington sashayed femininely into the hall, her cats Fiona, Errol, Annabelle, and Ratty darting rapidly between her feet, Madeleine slipped carefully out from between the sheets. This was not a simple task, for ten-year-old Hyacinth Hicklebee-Riyatulle and her pet ferret, Celery, were curled up at the foot of the bed. Hyacinth—or, as she preferred to be called, Hyhy— was notorious for her obnoxious behavior, as well as for her fear of being alone. Maneuvering cautiously on her tiptoes, Madeleine crept away from her bed and past that of thirteen-year-old Rhode Islander Lucy "Lulu" Punchalower.

Deep in slumber, with her strawberry blond hair covering her freckled face, Lulu displayed a softness she rarely exhibited when awake. The bold young girl was known for speaking without restraint, for never holding back a thought or a roll of the eyes. Of course, it ought to be mentioned that Lulu's confident façade instantly evaporated where confined spaces were concerned. When forced into an elevator or a room without windows, Lulu broke into unbridled hysteria. The young girl once went so far as to hijack a window washer's cart to avoid the elevator at a Boston hotel. Unfortunately, Lulu hadn't a clue how to maneuver the thing and had to be rescued by the fire department. The whole debacle wound up on the nightly news, much to the chagrin of her image-conscious parents.

Now, as the sun blazed above the dilapidated limestone mansion known as Summerstone, Madeleine tiptoed down the creaky stairs, the importance of the day that lay ahead weighing heavily on her mind. If Mrs. Wellington and Abernathy did not reconcile, and thereby undermine reporter Sylvie Montgomery's exposé, School of Fear would quickly and most unceremoniously cease to exist. And as nothing else had worked on her phobia, not even the terribly experimental seminar Brainwashing for Bugs, Madeleine couldn't afford to lose the school. This was a fact all the School of Fearians recognized: without the completion of the course, they could easily backslide into restricted, panic-filled lives.

By the time Madeleine dashed through the pink fleur-de-lis foyer and past Mrs. Wellington's wall of pageant photos, her stomach had twisted itself into a highly complicated Celtic knot. Even the sight of the Great Hall, a grand corridor of one-of-a-kind doors, couldn't distract Madeleine from her mounting anxiety. The airplane hatch, farm gate, giraffe-shaped portal, and countless other creative aberrations fell on blind eyes as she barreled into the ballroom, inside which both the classroom and drawing room were housed.

Immediately upon entering, Madeleine saw Mrs. Wellington, dressed in pink satin pajamas that perfectly matched her eye shadow, pacing nervously in front of the couch. Before her time at School of Fear, Madeleine had never known a woman who reapplied makeup before bed. But Mrs. Wellington was just such a woman and had on the eye shadow, rouge, false eyelashes, and lipstick to prove it.

"Shower Captain—thank Heavens you're *finally* here!" Mrs. Wellington exclaimed.

Madeleine delicately smoothed her clear plastic shower cap before looking up at the old woman with irritation. "Mrs. Wellington, I loathe to be impertinent on such a day, but you only asked me here thirty seconds ago. And please stop calling me Shower Captain. It makes me feel like a cartoon character—and not a very attractive one at that!"

"It appears someone woke up on the left side of the bed."

"I know I shouldn't ask," Madeleine said with a sigh, "but what's wrong with the left side of the bed?"

"It's not the *right* side of the bed," Mrs. Wellington said briskly as her mouth shifted colors. The old woman was a bit of a genetic anomaly, with oversized capillaries in her lips that darkened when she was angry, nervous, or embarrassed.

Madeleine abstained from responding, as she was nearing the end of her perfunctory spider-and-creepy crawler scan of the room. Web-free surroundings normally left the young girl feeling terribly relaxed, but not today. There was simply too much at stake for her to be relaxed. Why, just the thought of being relaxed felt downright irresponsible, almost illegal!

Mrs. Wellington gracefully lowered herself onto the couch, crossing her legs, and beckoned for Madeleine to do the same. As if performing a well-orchestrated dance, the four cats circled the woman's feet before falling into the sphinx pose. After carefully noting the locations of all four tails and sixteen paws, Madeleine took her place next to Mrs. Wellington, mimicking her teacher's perfectly vertical posture. As the young girl prepared to ask the nature of the early-morning visit, she focused on Mrs. Wellington's long, frail fingers, awash in brownish liver spots. It was dangerously easy to forget that beneath the powerful persona lurked a feeble body weathered by time and experiences.

"Madeleine, I asked you here today," Mrs. Wellington announced, "because something strange is happening to me."

"I'm quite sure I understand. The possibility of losing the school must be awfully frightening for you; it's a legacy you've worked so hard to maintain. And as for confronting Abernathy, well, I should think it's normal to be scared after all these years."

"Need I remind you that I am the headmistress of School of *Fear*? I know fright better than anyone! As a matter of fact, I recently awarded myself an honorary PhD in the subject, so I can assure you that *fear* is not the issue. It's something far more distressing," Mrs. Wellington said firmly as she grabbed her chest, contorted her face, and swallowed loudly.

"You're not going to fake your own death again, are you?"

"No!" Mrs. Wellington barked. Then she softened her tone, saying, "Please, Madeleine, I've come to you for your sensible British advice. I need help. Something is very, very wrong with me...."

"As sensible and British as I am, I think I ought to wake the others. After all, Theo is terribly adept at diagnosing people, and Garrison is strong should you need help walking, and Lulu knows CPR, and Hyacinth, well, she is actually the opposite of helpful, so perhaps I'll leave her and the ferret to sleep," Madeleine babbled uncontrollably, panic seeping into her voice, as she left the room to collect her friends.

Within minutes Madeleine had returned with her groggy and pajama-clad classmates—Theo, Garrison, and Lulu. A self-proclaimed specialist on both death and illness, thirteen-year-old New Yorker Theo Bartholomew maneuvered his pudgy frame to the front of the group. After a quick smoothing of his tousled brown locks, he pushed his smudged glasses up the shaft of his button-like nose and began his examination.

"The doctor is in," Theo announced confidently as he grabbed Mrs. Wellington's wrist. "And the good news is I feel a pulse, which means you are *definitely* still alive."

"Ugh, Maddie should never have woken you up," Lulu moaned, already annoyed by Theo's theatrics.

Rather surprisingly, Theo ignored Lulu, instead focusing all his attention on Mrs. Wellington. "Are you experiencing any sharp or dull pains in your head?"

"No," Mrs. Wellington responded. "I haven't had any problems up there since I stopped using tar as wig glue."

"In that case, I think I can rule out an advanced brain tumor, aneurysm, or cranial abscess," Theo declared matter-of-factly before continuing. "Have you experienced any tingling in your extremities?"

"My extremities?"

" 'Extremities' is just a fancy word for arms and legs," Madeleine explained.

"I'm looking for signs of a stroke, multiple sclerosis, fibromyalgia—just your basic run-of-the-mill, life-altering illnesses," Theo said.

"Honestly, half the time I forget I even have extremities, let alone feel them," answered Mrs. Wellington.

"Interesting," Theo said as he took off his grimy glasses and cleaned them on his pajama top.

"*Interesting*? Why is that *interesting*?" Mrs. Wellington asked impatiently.

"Oh, it isn't interesting at all. I just like to say that word. Now then, have you noticed any large portions of flesh disappearing from your body?"

"Most definitely not."

"So that's a no on flesh-eating bacteria," Theo said as he rubbed his chin and looked down at the felines lounging around Mrs. Wellington's feet. "Is there a chance one of the cats might have scratched you, given you a case of the old cat scratch fever?"

"Totally made-up disease," Lulu mumbled under her breath.

"Actually, Lulu, it's *totally real*," Theo said. "And if you don't believe me, go on iTunes—there's a song about it."

"Sorry, I forgot how credible iTunes is when diagnosing an illness," Lulu quipped.

"I assure you, Chubby, these cats haven't had a ragged nail a day in their life," Mrs. Wellington said. "Have you not seen the kitty spa in the basement? There's even an artificial tongue to groom their coats."

"I hate basements...no windows...bad news," Lulu muttered nervously to no one in particular.

"So that's a no on cat scratch fever, flesh-eating bacteria, brain tumor, aneurysm, cranial abscess, multiple sclerosis, stroke, and fibromyalgia. Well, I've got to say, I'm stumped. This might be one for the record books, or maybe just WebMD, but since we don't have Internet access, I'm going to have to go with medical mystery."

"Seriously?" said fourteen-year-old Miami native Garrison Feldman as he stepped in front of Theo. Tall and tanned, with shaggy blond hair, the water-phobic boy had an innately commanding presence. "Why don't you just tell us what's going on, Mrs. Wellington? I promise it will be a lot easier than letting Theo examine you."

Mrs. Wellington nodded and pursed her lips before

beginning. "Ever since I learned about Sylvie Montgomery's story and the plan for me to confront Abernathy, I've been having the weirdest sensations."

"What kind of sensations?" Lulu asked with mounting curiosity.

"Heaviness in my chest, tears in my eyes, a sinking feeling in my stomach. And worst of all, my thoughts keep returning to the past, back to when I first met Abernathy...."

More decades ago than a chimpanzee can count, a widower by the name of Mr. Wellington brought his son, Abernathy, to School of Fear. The boy was in desperate need of help due to a most irrational fear of stepmothers, also known as novercaphobia. But as fate would have it, Mrs. Wellington, then known as Ms. Hesterfield, and Mr. Wellington fell madly in love. Of course, they tried to hide their feelings from Abernathy, but he soon discovered their love letters, which sent him on a downward spiral. From that point on, Abernathy never spent another night under the same roof as his father or stepmother. Instead, he retreated to the great outdoors, choosing to live the quiet life of a recluse.

Greatly weathered by Mother Nature, these days Abernathy sported gray, leathery skin and ragged, sun-stained hair. However, his most notable attribute was a near complete inability to socialize normally. Had it not been for his profound but terribly undiscerning love of music, he would still be living among the trees and squirrels. Rather shockingly, it was the rapture of Hyacinth's tone-deaf singing that had lured Abernathy back to School of Fear. And once there, he grew rather fond of human company, having spent the last few decades engaged in one-sided conversations with forest animals.

"Contestants, you must tell me the truth," Mrs. Wellington now implored her students, or, as she saw them, "contestants in the beauty pageant of life." "What's wrong with me?"

"Am I the only one who thinks that's a loaded question?" Theo asked with a furrowed brow.

From the back of the ballroom came the unmistakable sound of Mrs. Wellington's manservant, Schmidty. In balancing his enormous polyester-covered belly and elaborate comb-over, Schmidty had developed a very distinctive shuffle.

"Madame, must I explain what's happening to you

again?" Schmidty called out from across the room, the portly English bulldog Macaroni waddling close behind in striped blue pajamas.

"It's not meningitis, is it?" Theo asked, stepping away from Mrs. Wellington. "Because my neck is already feeling a little sore."

"No, Mister Theo, it's something far more common.... Feelings," replied Schmidty.

"Don't listen to him; I've got plaque on my teeth smarter than he is!" Mrs. Wellington said indignantly.

"Okay, we definitely need to find a dentist who makes house calls," Lulu grumbled with unmistakable repulsion.

"Madame is experiencing emotions such as sorrow, regret, and melancholy for the first time in decades, and understandably she's rather overwhelmed," Schmidty explained as the old woman wiped away tears.

"Abernathy hates me," Mrs. Wellington muttered. "My own stepson despises me, and soon the whole world will know that I failed him as both a parent and a teacher. The school will close and there'll be nothing left for me in this life!"

"No way, Mrs. Wellington! We're not going to let that happen," Garrison stated confidently. "You and

17

Abernathy are going to work things out. It's like the Red Sox–Yankees rivalry; it's time for this to end. And once it does, we'll show Sylvie Montgomery that her information is wrong, and she'll have no choice but to kill the story."

At that moment, a light snorting sound reverberated through the room, coming from the far window. At first no one paid it any mind, but as the sniffing grew heavier, Mrs. Wellington turned her head in curiosity.

"The pig is back!" the old woman screamed, deftly jumping to her feet and grabbing a nearby lamp and flinging it at the window.

CHAPTER 2

EVERYONE'S AFRAID OF SOMETHING:

Swinophobia is the fear

of pigs or swine.

Not only did Sylvie Montgomery sound like a pig, she also very much resembled a member of the swine family. Her rosy complexion, drooping midsection, and dome-shaped derriere, complete with a protruding tailbone, were rather striking. But in truth it was her nose, thick and bulbous, that cemented her piglike appearance. Her nose dominated her face, making it nearly impossible to notice any of Sylvie's other features. But she didn't mind, for that swollen spherical snout was her secret weapon. It alerted her to the presence of classified information, which Sylvie then tenaciously went after, relentlessly digging until she got to the bottom of the story. And with a mere three weeks until her article was to go to press, Sylvie was determined to uncover every last fact about Mrs. Wellington, Abernathy, and the school on the hill.

As Sylvie peeked through the window of the school, the lamp Mrs. Wellington had hurled in her direction crashed to the floor with such thunder that Schmidty and the students actually shrieked. Sylvie withdrew from the window, waddling quickly away before Mrs. Wellington could lob anything else at her.

"Might I suggest using a tad more emotional control when meeting with Abernathy?" Madeleine said delicately to Mrs. Wellington.

"But you've got to admit she's got pretty good aim for an old lady," Lulu noted admiringly.

"Spoken like a true juvenile delinquent," Theo replied judgmentally to Lulu, who rather expectedly rolled her eyes in response.

"Come on, we better get dressed. Abernathy will be up soon," Garrison said to Lulu, Theo, and Madeleine, while Mrs. Wellington and Schmidty remained seated in the drawing room.

"I can't believe Abernathy's sleeping in the basement," Madeleine said, shaking her head in disbelief.

"Um, hello? The kitty spa is down there. I bet that place is pure luxury. Plus, there's the artificial cat tongue," Theo said excitedly as the group made their way into the Great Hall.

As the pudgy-cheeked boy pondered the mechanics of building a synthetic tongue, Madeleine fretted over her clothing options for the day ahead. She had watched enough C-SPAN to know that the Abernathy-Wellington summit warranted a smart outfit. However, just as she decided on a navy dress with white piping, the sound of glass fracturing erupted through the Great Hall. After exchanging tense glances, the foursome dashed down the remainder of the corridor and into the foyer. There they were met with a rather disturbing sight: Abernathy smashing one of Mrs. Wellington's famed pageant photos with his heel. The gangly, gray-skinned man had a permanent hunch from staring at his feet, and in his old flannel shirt and dirty jeans, Abernathy appeared very much out of place amid the grandiosity of Summerstone.

"Abernathy, what on earth are you doing?" Madeleine asked as her blood pressure skyrocketed. The girl had yet to brush her teeth, and already the day was spinning wildly out of control.

"Oh, my bad. I bumped into the wall by accident," Abernathy said in his squeaky, high-pitched voice. Although the many years of living in the forest had prematurely aged him, his voice remained that of a boy on the cusp of puberty.

"*My bad*? People who have spent decades in the forest don't say *my bad*," Theo scoffed to the others. "I think he's been holing up at the Ramada Inn off the interstate, watching cable television and ordering room service. This whole thing is one big con!"

"Actually, Celery taught him that. Pretty cool, right?" Hyacinth said as she bounded down the last of the stairs wearing her ubiquitous pantsuit and with her ferret perched on her shoulder. "And FYI, Celery and I are pretty peeved at you guys for deserting us. You know how much we hate to wake up alone! Besties don't leave besties, remember? Do I need to sing the 'Besties Forever' song again?"

"Oh, that would be lovely," replied Abernathy, the sole person ever eager to hear Hyacinth's off-key voice.

"Unfortunately, I think there is a slightly more pressing issue at hand," Madeleine said seriously.

"Breakfast? I couldn't agree more," Theo replied.

"No," Lulu answered. "We need to hide that picture before Mrs. Wellington sees it. This is not how we want to start the reconciliation."

"I'm really sorry, guys," Abernathy chirped, staring intently at his feet. "It was an involuntary reaction. Sort of like when you see a squirrel about to get run over by a car and you dart into the street to save him. It just felt like the right thing to do."

"Squirrel-cide is a terrible thing to see," Theo lamented dramatically.

"I hate...*her*," Abernathy growled as he focused on another of Mrs. Wellington's portraits on the wall. A bitter and angry expression overtook his ashen face. Much like a wild animal, he appeared to be running on instincts alone. It was hard to believe that this was the same man who only moments earlier had spoken timidly of rescuing a hypothetical squirrel.

"Well, this should be a piece of cake," Lulu said sarcastically. "I don't know what we were worried about."

"Um, Abernathy refusing to forgive Mrs. Wellington, ruining any and all chances of saving the school," Theo responded earnestly, then paused before saying, "Oh, wait—that was a rhetorical question, wasn't it?"

Two hours passed before Mrs. Wellington was finally prepared to meet Abernathy face-to-face in the ballroom. For the occasion, she donned a bright yellow dress and petticoat along with a soaring feathered cap. Schmidty worried that she looked a great deal like Big Bird from *Sesame Street*, but didn't have the heart to tell her as much. Of course, it certainly didn't help that her makeup, applied by the legally blind Schmidty, perfectly matched her outfit.

In preparation for the morning summit, Mrs. Wellington demanded that Schmidty make actual Casu Frazigu, also known as maggot cheese. Ever since the cheese had been outlawed for a wide variety of health reasons, he had merely flavored food to taste of Casu Frazigu. However, sensing the fragility of her mood,

Schmidty decided it best not to argue. Instead, he tricked Mrs. Wellington by using overcooked granules of rice as a stand-in for maggots.

Believing the Casu Frazigu to be real, Lulu, Theo, Garrison, and Madeleine inched away from the vile delicacy. Theo even went so far as to move the snacks he had brought away from the cheese, worried that an overactive maggot might make the jump.

As the students huddled around the table, Mrs. Wellington, Schmidty, and Macaroni sat stoically on the couch. While waiting for Hyacinth to return with Abernathy, her personal singing companion, Garrison took a moment to remind his peers of the plan.

"As soon as Abernathy enters, I want everyone smiling at him. We need to make him feel welcome," Garrison whispered. "And remember, be patient—we can't just jump right into the whole 'you guys need to work this out' speech. First we need to say hello, make some small talk, maybe even have a snack—"

"Let's not forget who brought the non–Casu Frazigu snacks: me!" Theo interrupted while literally reaching his arm around to pat himself on the back.

"But these aren't the most mature people; it's rather

plausible they might immediately start yelling," Madeleine said perceptively. "In truth, there's really no telling what they'll do."

"If they get rowdy, I say we break out some Styrofoam bats and just let them go at it," Lulu added.

"I don't think so," Garrison quickly countered.

"Um, don't knock it; we did it in family therapy," Lulu said in response.

"With all due respect, Lulu, from what we've heard of your family, the exercise doesn't appear to have been terribly effective," Madeleine assessed candidly.

"Yeah, I guess you have a point. But it was really fun, one of the best times of my life," Lulu said, staring wistfully off into space.

The faint sound of Abernathy and Hyacinth singing Christmas carols suddenly rippled through the ballroom, instantly grabbing everyone's attention.

"Mister Abernathy certainly enjoys Christmas tunes," Schmidty said with a nervous smile, and Macaroni tilted his head at the sound of the tonally challenged duo.

"A terribly odd affinity considering he's Jewish," Mrs. Wellington mumbled. "He had a bar mitzvah and everything."

"Being open to other faiths is a wonderful quality," Madeleine offered optimistically.

"About that bar mitzvah: Did he get a lot of gifts? Not that I am basing my conversion to any religion on the gift-to-child ratio. However, there is no denying that eight days of Hanukkah to one day of Christmas is pretty compelling," Theo said emphatically.

"Trust me, no one thinks you're picking a religion based on gifts," Lulu said with a roll of her eyes. "We all know it's coming down to the food: Who has the best, and the most of it?"

As Theo prepared a retort, the tone-deaf twosome entered the ballroom. They were met with six tense faces—seven if they counted Macaroni. Instantly unnerved by the room's many scrutinizing eyes, Abernathy trailed off while staring keenly at his shoes. In stark contrast, Hyacinth continued to sing with all the enthusiasm of a Broadway star on opening night.

"Miss Hyacinth," Schmidty said loudly, "perhaps now would be a good time to rest your vocal cords."

"I go by Hyhy, remember? I know you're old and could die at any second, but we're still besties, and besties call me Hyhy!"

"Thank you for those extremely uplifting words, Miss *Hyhy*," Schmidty replied drolly.

"Hey, Abernathy," Garrison jumped in, offering the biggest smile humanly possible. "How are you? How's everything going?"

Abernathy continued to stare at his shoes, seemingly oblivious to Garrison's greeting. Undeterred, Garrison turned toward Mrs. Wellington, once again offering a massive smile.

"Mrs. Wellington, how are you? You look really...yellow. I mean, *nice in yellow*," Garrison rambled awkwardly.

For the first time in her life, Mrs. Wellington ignored a compliment and remained totally and utterly silent. Everyone in the room quickly grew ill at ease, inadvertently setting the stage for Theo, who cleared his throat in an embarrassingly theatrical manner. It sounded like a cat with laryngitis trying to dislodge a hairball.

"As the MC—that's master of ceremonies, for those of you not up-to-date on your acronyms—I would like to welcome you—"

"Wait a minute. No one made you master of ceremonies," Lulu interrupted Theo.

"Let's not get caught up in details, Lulu. Now, as I was saying, I brought sourdough bread, cookies, scones, and crackers. That's right, people, I am talking about carbohydrates! And I think we can all agree that if carbohydrates were a religion we'd convert—"

"Theo, if I may interrupt, I feel we're getting wildly off course here. This is about Abernathy and Mrs. Wellington," Madeleine said, adjusting her shower cap.

"As usual, Maddie's right," Garrison agreed, unintentionally strengthening the young girl's lingering crush on him. "Mrs. Wellington, Abernathy, let's just sit down and talk about this like adults, or at the very least like angry ballplayers."

"Celery wants me to point out that we're not *technically* adults."

"How many times do I have to tell you that thirteen is considered a man in many cultures?" Theo asked with frustration. "And the fact that I am not a member of any of these cultures does not make it any less true."

"Sorry. Celery and I are super age-conscious now that we're in the double digits. Actually, don't say anything," Hyacinth said, putting her hands over the ferret's

31

ears, "but she's only four. I don't have the heart to tell her that she's still in the single digits in human years. You know how desperate she is to fit in."

"And you said *I* was off-topic? She's talking about a ferret with an identity crisis," Theo huffed to Madeleine.

Up to this point, both Mrs. Wellington and Abernathy had successfully managed to avoid even the slightest eye contact. Abernathy was still very content staring at his shoes, while Mrs. Wellington dabbed her misty eyes with a monogrammed pink handkerchief.

"Mrs. Wellington," Garrison said kindly, "I know this is hard, but someone needs to start this conversation. You're the teacher; what do you say you give it a shot?"

"Yes, I suppose I could do that," Mrs. Wellington replied, trembling with emotion.

The mere sound of her voice ignited a burning sensation in Abernathy's toes, which quickly rose through his body. As the heat reached his head, he lifted his eyes and looked at Mrs. Wellington for the first time. His face flashed red, his eyes narrowed, and his lips quivered. Then, in a wholly unexpected turn of events, Abernathy began to growl at the old woman.

The raw emotion that had plagued Mrs. Wellington all day quickly evaporated as her stern aloofness returned. It appeared both parties were falling back into their long-held dynamic of hostility.

"How dare you growl at me? I am the headmistress of this school, as well as your stepmother, and as such demand to be treated with respect!" Mrs. Wellington spat out harshly.

"Let's not jump to conclusions," Theo said to Mrs. Wellington. "That was probably just Abernathy's stomach; after all, he's been eating twigs and beetles for decades. I'm sure he has a wide variety of gastric intestinal issues."

"That wasn't my stomach, young boy," Abernathy responded quietly to Theo.

"Young *man*," Theo corrected Abernathy.

"I meant no offense—well, not to you anyway. Just *her*."

"How dare you call me *her*?" Mrs. Wellington snapped.

"I suppose *it* would be more appropriate."

"I will have you know that only this morning some-one mistook me for a woman of twenty."

"Madame, it hardly counts when that someone is you," Schmidty interjected from a few feet away.

Paying Schmidty and the others no mind, Abernathy once again started to growl. As his tone grew more guttural, Mrs. Wellington countered by hissing with the ferocity of a feral feline.

"You are both far too old to behave in such an undignified manner," Madeleine interjected. "Now, I'm sure we can solve this civilly, over a cup of tea."

"And some cheese sandwiches," Theo added.

Still staring intently at Mrs. Wellington, Abernathy bared his green-tinted teeth and snarled.

"Celery thinks we should tell Abernathy about whitening toothpaste. It's probably not available in the forest," Hyacinth offered in her usual peppy tone.

"Would anyone care for a cookie, or a piece of bread?" Madeleine asked with a cracking voice, desperate to distract Abernathy from Mrs. Wellington and vice versa. "Theo is right; we all think much more clearly on a full stomach."

"That's why fat people are so smart," Theo interjected proudly. "As a matter of fact, I think I'll title my memoir *Full Stomach: How Food Made Me Fun, Fabulous, and Fierce.*"

Ignoring Theo, Madeleine approached Abernathy with the tray of food. Much to everyone's delight, he picked up a cookie. Eating was most definitely a good sign—or at least that's what they thought before he jettisoned the cookie at Mrs. Wellington, knocking her wig askew in the process.

"Cookie down," Theo whimpered quietly to himself as he mourned the loss of the sugary treat.

Mrs. Wellington corrected her wig while seething over the indignity of the situation. She then grabbed a piece of bread and lobbed it directly at Abernathy's gray face.

"In case you've forgotten, there are starving children in Africa, and maybe even one in here, so put down the food," Theo said with the seriousness of a hostage negotiator.

"I told you we needed Styrofoam bats," Lulu called out to Garrison as the action escalated.

Much like in a war zone, artillery was firing so rapidly that one could hardly keep track of who was lobbing what. The air was a veritable sea of cookies, bread, crackers, and crumbs. Once the food was finished, the floor literally covered in culinary casualties, Mrs. Wellington grabbed the jug of milk and splashed it directly into her stepson's gray face. As milk dripped slowly down his body, the old woman cackled evilly, prompting Abernathy to grab the sole remaining item on the table, the Casu Frazigu, and smash it into her yellow-makeup-covered face.

Both Abernathy and Mrs. Wellington had abruptly transformed into coldhearted warriors, leaving behind absolutely no sign of the sheepish man or weepy woman from before.

"Get it together!" Garrison screamed judgmentally at the soggy twosome. "You guys are grown-ups."

As Mrs. Wellington brushed large chunks of Casu Frazigu off her yellow dress, she looked crossly at Abernathy and muttered, "Barbarian."

"Mrs. Wellington, need I remind you that you are the teacher in this room?" Madeleine asked disdainfully.

"Not anymore," Garrison added. "As of right now, Mrs. Wellington and Abernathy are the students and *we're* the teachers."

"What a day!" Theo said excitedly. "First an MC and now a teacher; my résumé is pretty much building itself."

"This isn't Cuba, contestants," Mrs. Wellington snapped. "Coups are illegal."

"Mrs. Wellington, you can either accept us as your and Abernathy's teachers or lose everything you've worked for; the choice is yours," Madeleine stated firmly.

After a few seconds, the Casu Frazigu–drenched woman nodded her head in agreement. Madeleine then offered Lulu a knowing glance. The freckle-faced girl turned to Abernathy, who had once again averted his eyes.

"Abernathy, unless you want to wind up as some circus freak being hunted by the media like Bigfoot," Lulu said with certainty, "you need to do what we say, got it?"

Abernathy quickly nodded his head in agreement, clearly terrified at the idea of being exploited by the press. All eyes, except Abernathy's, then turned to Garrison for the details of the plan. Feeling an enormous amount of pressure, the tanned boy began to sweat as he did when presented with an ocean, lake, or pool view. After receiving a reassuring smile and a nod of the head from Schmidty, Garrison quickly wiped his upper lip, shook off his doubts, and rose to the occasion.

"Let's keep this simple," Garrison declared. "Abernathy needs a makeover both mentally and physically, so he can appear *somewhat* normal. And if we can't actually get him to forgive Mrs. Wellington, we'll work on getting him to pretend long enough to undermine Sylvie Montgomery's story."

"Celery's worried the plan sounds a little vague," Hyacinth squeaked sprightly.

"Hyacinth, much like your sense of tact, I'm sure details are forthcoming," Madeleine said coldly.

As Hyacinth whispered animatedly into her ferret's ear, Theo quietly muttered out of the side of his mouth, "What about the old woman?"

"I think Lulu may have been on to something with the Styrofoam bats," Garrison responded half-jokingly, still unsure how to handle the opposing personalities of Mrs. Wellington and Abernathy.

CHAPTER 3

EVERYONE'S AFRAID OF SOMETHING:

Coulrophobia is the fear

of clowns.

Continuing in his natural role as leader, Garrison designated an area of expertise for each student. It would not be easy to smooth Abernathy's rough edges while also mending his highly fractured relationship with Mrs. Wellington, but the students had no choice but to try. After all, Mrs. Wellington was more than a friend and teacher; she was the sole person who had ever helped them with their fears.

Madeleine was assigned to academic tutoring, most

notably world events Abernathy missed while living in the forest. The globally minded girl realized she had her work cut out for her when Abernathy mentioned the Berlin Wall and the U.S.S.R. in *present tense*. It appeared that while living among the trees and squirrels, far from newspapers, television, or radio, the man had missed the 1989 fall of the Berlin Wall and the 1991 dissolution of the U.S.S.R. But perhaps even more jarring than missed world events was his technological illiteracy. The gray-skinned man had never seen a cell phone or a BlackBerry, nor had he heard of the Internet.

As for Abernathy's physical appearance, self-proclaimed fashionista Theo demanded to be in charge of overhauling his wardrobe. Basic social skills such as eye contact and small talk fell to Lulu. While she herself lacked a great many social graces, Garrison believed her tough personality would be an asset in breaking through to Abernathy. Hyacinth was designated the man's on-call singing partner, while Garrison was to handle sports. The athletically inclined boy held firm that all normal American males had a basic understanding of baseball, basketball, or football. Much to Theo's annoyance, Garrison refused to add figure skating to that list.

As for greasing the wheels of friendship between Abernathy and Mrs. Wellington, the details were much cruder, even—dare one say it?—fuzzy. The feeble plan consisted of group-therapy and hypnosis sessions led by Schmidty. While the comb-over–topped man lacked any psychological or hypnotic credentials, he offered his services, and considering the options, the students blindly accepted.

"I don't think we should do this without a proper plan name. Maybe 'Mrs. Wellington and Abernathy Get Their Groove Back,' or 'Project Groove' for short," Theo said while enjoying a Casu Frazigu–free lunch of grilled cheese sandwiches and green beans with Madeleine, Lulu, Garrison, Hyacinth, and Schmidty. Mrs. Wellington and Abernathy had both chosen to eat in their rooms to avoid each other.

"Oh my gosh! Yes! We should make matching tee shirts, too," Hyacinth said excitedly.

"No plan name, no tee shirts. We don't need any more distractions, got it?" Lulu responded firmly to Theo and Hyacinth.

"If I were a police officer, I would arrest you for killing a good time," Theo retorted dramatically.

"Whatever. You'll be thanking me for keeping us on track when we pull this off," Lulu answered.

"Schmidty, I certainly am not trying to criticize your housekeeping skills, for I understand you are both visually challenged and, well, rather mature, but have you seen the state of the windows in here?" Madeleine asked, pointing to the smudged glass.

"Miss Madeleine, it's Sylvie's snout," Schmidty said with a dejected sigh. "She appears to have pressed it against every window at Summerstone. It shall take me years to clean them all."

"Or you could die first?" Hyacinth added. "That's the upside to death: no more cleaning."

"Again, Miss Hyacinth, thank you for those inspiring words," Schmidty responded sarcastically.

"I know that you're old, but as you have been told, call me Hyhy! Call me Hyhy!" Hyacinth sang atrociously.

"I'm pretty sure my ears just tried to kill themselves," Lulu deadpanned to Hyacinth.

"I'm totally fine with your joke, but Celery says to watch it, or she'll chew your face off while you sleep," Hyacinth shot back with her usual perky smile.

"I think you should remind your ferret that Theo may be a vegetarian, but *I'm* not," Lulu replied before breaking into a most disturbing grin.

Shortly after lunch Madeleine arranged her tutoring station in the Fearnasium. Nestled between life-size clowns who cackled when their noses were squeezed and an extensive collection of animal skulls, Madeleine set up a small table and chairs. Once seated, she noticed a mobile of Chihuahuas dangling directly above her. It was an adorable visual, clearly left over from a student suffering from a fear of small dogs, also known as microcynophobia. And while Madeleine would normally have performed a closer inspection of the miniatures, she was already far too preoccupied with her role as educator.

"Abernathy, I am going to begin with a few simple

facts regarding today's world leaders. Please repeat after me: Barack Obama is the president of the United States of America."

"Barack Obama is the president of the United States of America."

Madeleine smiled, already pleased with herself, and now with her pupil.

"David Cameron is the prime minister of the United Kingdom."

"David Cameron is the prime minister of the United Kingdom."

"Nicolas Sarkozy is the president of France."

"Mrs. Wellington is the destroyer of children's dreams."

"Abernathy!" Madeleine gasped and pulled down on her shower cap in shock.

"What?" the man asked softly. "Isn't that what you said?"

"I most certainly did *not* say that!"

"But you wanted to...."

"I did not! Mrs. Wellington does *not* destroy children's dreams; on the contrary, she helps us achieve our dreams. Perhaps her tactics are a bit unorthodox, at times even illegal, but you must believe me, she can help you. If not for that woman, I would still be dressed in a veil and a belt of repellents."

Suddenly a voice erupted from one of the clowns, causing both Abernathy and Madeleine to squeal with fright.

"Maddie, Maddie, Maddie."

Madeleine quickly recognized the voice as Theo's, prompting her to sigh with extreme annoyance. The boy awkwardly pushed his way out from behind the clown, accidentally squeezing its nose in the process, setting off a terribly wicked cackle. So grim and evil was the sound that all present developed a slight touch of coulrophobia.

"Madeleine," Theo said, strutting with a great deal of misplaced bravado, "not that I was eavesdropping, but remember, a hall monitor is always on duty."

"I highly doubt that spying is part of your official hall-monitor duties," Madeleine replied with visible irritation.

"Talking about your lack of a veil while wearing a shower cap isn't the best line of reasoning," Theo said, playing awkwardly with the sash across his chest.

"I disagree wholeheartedly. Relapse is a well-known

part of recovery. Plus, I cannot believe that you would say anything about my cap, knowing what I went through with that ghastly Balinese spider!"

Abernathy watched Theo and Madeleine with great attention; it had been a long time since he had seen people argue up close. He forgot how engaging other people's problems could be. It reminded him a bit of watching television. Of course, the last time Abernathy watched TV there were only ten channels, and they were all black-and-white.

"Someone call NASA—your spider scar is glowing," Theo said animatedly while looking at the now-red indentation on Madeleine's forehead.

"It's like a spider stencil," Abernathy said softly, utterly transfixed by the mark.

The mere reminder of the arachnid roadkill sent Madeleine rushing out of the room, on the brink of vomiting. The girl had always had a sensitive stomach where spiders and insects were concerned.

"Was it something I said?" Abernathy asked meekly as the Fearnasium door clanged shut.

"Yeah, probably," Theo said absentmindedly as he realized the great opportunity that had just presented itself. "Did I ever tell you about the time Mrs. Wellington faked her own death? It was amazing!"

"That does sound amazing—well, except for the *fake* part," Abernathy responded eerily.

Theo looked around the Fearnasium, from clowns to reptile heads to turn-of-the-century needles, and felt a shiver run up his spine.

"Before I rethink the whole 'I'm not afraid to be alone with you' stance, please tell me you're kidding."

"I'm kidding," Abernathy said unconvincingly.

"Okay, good. Because if there is one thing I don't like in a friend, it's homicidal urges," Theo explained, wiping his brow. "As I was saying, most teachers would never bother to fake their own deaths to get a bunch of kids to confront their fears. Of course, there are some sound reasons for that. After all, I was pretty traumatized by the experience; I barely spoke or ate for twenty-four hours...." Theo trailed off before catching sight of Abernathy's horrified expression.

"Can you just forget I said anything?" Theo asked Abernathy with raised eyebrows.

It appeared there was a bit more to teaching than either Madeleine or Theo had expected.

That night at dinner Mrs. Wellington and Abernathy were seated as far away from each other as possible while still actually being in the same room. While no food was thrown, there was palpable tension in the air. After exactly thirteen minutes of silence, Abernathy looked up at Mrs. Wellington and growled.

"Oh, save it for the coyotes, nature boy! That doesn't scare me!"

"Are there coyotes up here? A little warning would have been nice," Theo said, his mouth full of food.

"You're so ugly you give me a stomachache," Abernathy said awkwardly to Mrs. Wellington, stumbling over his words.

"Actually, that's probably the Casu Frazigu," Theo responded, his mouth still full of food.

"Unless someone's hair is on fire or Sylvie is at the window, do not speak with food in your mouth," Lulu said strictly. "You're on the verge of ruining my appetite...like, forever."

"Abernathy," Garrison said nicely, "if your comebacks were a baseball team, they would be the Pittsburgh Pirates. And that is not a good thing. I think you need a comeback intervention; maybe we can even do a joint one with you and Theo."

Mrs. Wellington narrowed her eyes at Garrison and whispered, "Judas." Luckily, Garrison hadn't a clue that Judas was the apostle who betrayed Jesus. As a matter of fact, Garrison didn't realize she'd said Judas. From his perspective he was rather certain she had said "nudist." Of course, he hadn't a clue what that meant, either.

"Excuse me," Theo said after carefully swallowing all his food. "Gary, did it ever occur to you that Abernathy and I have trouble stringing together biting comebacks because we're so kind? I mean, my heart is basically made of chocolate, i.e., the sweetest thing on earth."

Hyacinth leaned close to her ferret and listened, nodding her head. "Celery says you need an anatomy lesson because it's not your heart that's made of chocolate, but your stomach and thighs...."

"That was below the belt. And I mean that both literally and figuratively," Theo said dramatically, banging his fists on the table.

"She once hit me with a belt," Abernathy mumbled, staring meanly at Mrs. Wellington.

"What?" Lulu gasped. "That is just plain wrong."

"It was an imaginary belt!" Mrs. Wellington snapped defensively.

"It still hurt!"

"Oh, really? I doubt it hurt more than being arrested at the altar after my future stepson told the FBI I was responsible for the Kennedy assassination!"

"I warned you not to go through with the wedding! We were happy before you! You made me break my promise! You ruined everything!" Abernathy screamed before storming out of the room, his gray face now red with anger.

"What promise is he referring to?" Madeleine inquired sensibly.

"Oh, who knows? The man is straight out of a strait-jacket! Completely nutty!" Mrs. Wellington snapped with blood-red lips.

"Celery thinks we're in a lot of trouble," Hyacinth added with her usual peppy smile as the others digested the prickly situation.

"I never thought I'd say this," Lulu admitted quietly to herself, "but Celery's right."

Early the next morning, with dawn breaking outside, Lulu woke from a ghastly nightmare of being buried alive. The young girl had been locked in a wooden coffin, lowered six feet beneath the ground, and covered in pounds of dirt. In the midst of clawing at the box, splinters ravaging her hands, Lulu was jolted back to consciousness. Almost immediately, thoughts of elevators, bathrooms without windows, and underground parking garages crept into her mind. In order to avoid such places indefinitely, she would have to move to a remote corner of the world.

As Lulu felt herself regress emotionally, a highly derogatory chorus echoed through the bedroom. Already mired in frustration, the strawberry blond threw back her comforter and dashed across the hall to the spare room.

"The old lady in the wig is a pig, she's grim and dim and full of sin!" Abernathy and Hyacinth sang cheerfully in the extra bedroom.

"Hyacinth!" Lulu barked. "What are you doing? You're supposed to be helping the team, not hurting us!"

"Don't be mad, bossy bestie! It was Abernathy's idea. I wasn't so sure, but then he convinced Celery, and you know how hard it is to say no to a ferret with a harmonica."

"Wait a minute," Theo interrupted from behind Lulu in the upstairs hall. "Are you saying Celery can play the harmonica? I may be interested in starting a band with you guys, although I'll have to insist on top billing."

"Celery says dream on, Fatty."

"Theo! Stay focused! We are on the verge of losing everything, or haven't you noticed?" Lulu shrieked before stomping back to the girls' room and slamming the door.

Shrouded in embarrassment after being publicly chastised, Theo returned to the boys' room, where he promptly laid out his clothes: plaid shorts, a pastel polo shirt, and his trusty fanny pack. However, upon the removal of his pajama top, Theo froze. While not intuitive or even terribly perceptive, the boy felt something was amiss; he just didn't know what it was....

CHAPTER 4

EVERYONE'S AFRAID OF SOMETHING:

Pocrescophobia is the fear

of gaining weight.

The Duel of the Senses

I'm finished!" Theo shrieked to Schmidty as he stormed into the dining room. "Destroyed! Ruined! Obliterated! Demolished—"

"Yes," Schmidty interrupted. "I'm quite sure I get the point."

"Sylvie Montgomery's annihilated my career!"

"But you're only thirteen; you haven't got a career. To my knowledge you've never even been hired to babysit."

"Um, hello? I'm a hall monitor, only the most important

job at my school. Okay, maybe not the *most* important job at school, but definitely the most important job in the hallway."

"Of course." Schmidty nodded patronizingly. "A most significant position. However, I still don't understand what any of this has to do with Sylvie Montgomery."

"She was hiding in the tree outside my room and she snapped a *topless* photo of me. My career's finished!"

"But Mister Theo, you're a *boy*."

"You don't understand. No one at school knows I've got a tummy," Theo said as he pointed to his protruding midsection.

"Unless you've transferred to the Stevie Wonder School for the Visually Impaired, I assure you, they know," Schmidty stated categorically, looking at the boy's bulging belly.

"There's a little more to the story," Theo admitted meekly. "I've been wearing a girdle. I had no choice; no one likes fat people in power!"

"Mister Theo, some of the greatest politicians of our time have had large stomachs. Why, just think of Winston Churchill. And for the record, I've always found tummies rather distinguished," Schmidty added, pulling his polyester pants over the behemoth mass known as his stomach.

"Schmidty, I'm worried," Theo said quietly. "I don't know if we're going to be able to do this. Abernathy, Sylvie, and Mrs. Wellington are each so impossible."

"Oh, don't be pessimistic. Our lessons have just begun. Why, I haven't even tried hypnosis on them yet."

"Schmidty, I went to see the top three hypnotists in New York City. These are the people congressmen and athletes go to for big problems, and it still didn't work. I don't think waving a spoon in front of Abernathy's face is going to cut it."

"I was planning on using a pocket watch," Schmidty replied softly, clearly rattled by Theo's dour assessment. "We mustn't lose faith, Mister Theo. It's terribly important that we believe in our ability to do this, or else... we're sunk."

Theo smiled halfheartedly, more for Schmidty's sake than his own.

"Now, if you'll excuse me, Mister Theo, there is a pesky reporter out there who deserves a piece of my mind!"

"Okay, but don't give her too much; there's not a lot left."

Unfortunately, try as Schmidty did, he simply could not locate Sylvie Montgomery anywhere on the grounds. Of course, seeing as he's legally blind, the odds were rather unfavorably against him. Having neither heard a snort nor seen a splash of pink, Schmidty returned to the manse to conduct his first group-therapy session. After Theo's grave assessment of the scenario, he decided there simply wasn't time for traditional talking; something much bolder was required. However, outside of his hairdo, Schmidty was not a bold man. And so he sought the counsel of the boldest person he knew — Lulu. Fueled by the seemingly dire straits, she quickly devised a medieval-inspired game aimed at releasing pent-up aggression.

The Duel of the Senses, as Lulu called it, was to take place on the polo field off the Great Hall. Murals of bucolic rolling hills with white picket fences adorned the walls, while lush green AstroTurf covered the floor. Two of Mrs. Wellington's taxidermied horses were positioned face-to-face in the center of the room. A safe distance away, Theo, Madeleine, Hyacinth, Garrison, and Macaroni sat patiently in a row of chairs. Most abnormally, the students and Macaroni were covered head to toe in slimy, heat-sensitive Greenland Fungus. Mrs. Wellington kept the rare organism in a room off the Great Hall, as it was frighteningly easy to spread; one only had to touch it to be instantly mummified in the green goo.

The sound of Schmidty's poor trumpet playing signaled the start of the duel. Lulu led a trash bag–ensconced Mrs. Wellington to a regal black horse while Schmidty guided an equally trash bag–clad Abernathy to a spotted brown and white horse. Unfortunately, both were slippery and struggled to mount the stationary animals, an unforeseen consequence of their armor.

"Celery wants to know why we're covered in this nasty green stuff," Hyacinth whispered to Garrison. "I mean, I totally don't care, but you know how persnickety ferrets can be—they're total drama queens about their wardrobe."

"It blocks the smell," Garrison answered absent-mindedly from beneath his green sheen.

"The smell of what?"

"You *really* don't want to know."

Meanwhile, on the field, Lulu and Schmidty handed identical satchels to Abernathy and Mrs. Wellington before slowly backing away. The duel leaders then touched Macaroni, allowing the heat-sensitive fungus to spread to their bodies.

"May the best lunatic win," Lulu announced with a smirk before waving a pink paisley scarf in the air to officially start the Duel of the Senses.

The rules were simple: whoever stayed atop his or her horse the longest won. While remaining mounted on a taxidermied animal might sound simple, that certainly was not the case, for inside the identical satchels were small vats of foulness from the Library of Smelly Foods, which Mrs. Wellington and Abernathy were to strategically hurl at each other. Fainting, uncontrolled tremors, and violent vomiting are just some of the reported side effects from coming into contact with such items.

As Mrs. Wellington lobbed rotten cauliflower twice regurgitated by a guppy fish at Abernathy, Lulu explained the cost of losing to her classmates: the loser had to recall one kind memory about the winner, or eat every last ounce of rotten food off the floor.

Abernathy immediately proved a worthy opponent, ducking just in the nick of time to avoid the putrid blob of cauliflower. He then quickly tossed a mound of rotten roe, also known as fish eggs, at Mrs. Wellington's chest. The small green balls separated from the mass, sending a minimum of four roe directly up her nose. This incited the game's first occurrence of projectile vomiting.

"What an absolutely barbaric sport," Madeleine stated candidly to Theo as she shielded her eyes from the unsavory scene.

"I know. I think Lulu may have found her calling."

Mrs. Wellington slowly lifted her head off the back of the horse before shifting into a warrior pose. With the skill and ferocity of a Viking, the old woman attacked, sending putrid kimchi with her right hand and durian fruits with her left. The result was nothing short of an atomic olfactory bomb, knocking the breath right out of Abernathy. The gray-faced man wobbled back and forth a minimum of six times before collapsing abruptly onto the AstroTurf floor.

Mrs. Wellington neither cheered nor rejoiced in her victory. On the contrary, she appeared almost pained by the sight of her debilitated stepson. As she stood over Abernathy, carefully plugging her nose, the noxious-smelling man opened his eyes. Mrs. Wellington waited with bated breath, desperate to know what Abernathy would share.

"I'll eat the remnants," Abernathy declared defiantly, eradicating all sprigs of optimism from the room.

Mrs. Wellington nodded and turned to leave, then paused.

"When I was just your teacher, before you knew of my feelings for your father or his feelings for me, you told me you would never go back on your word, and to my knowledge you never have, but perhaps just this once you ought to."

Whether Abernathy did in fact eat the remnants of rotten cauliflower, kimchi, and durian fruit will never be known by anyone other than himself. Following Mrs. Wellington's proclamation, Schmidty and the students hurried out, desperate to wash away the slimy Greenland Fungus with a salt shower.

After thoroughly bathing in tomato juice, the sole substance capable of removing the stench of rotten food,

Abernathy set off for his first lesson in social graces. Lulu was to focus on the man's hunched shoulders, rapidly moving eye contact, and extremely awkward body language. Beyond passing Sylvie Montgomery's test, Lulu fretted that Abernathy's behavior left him ripe to be recruited by a cult.

"Abernathy, it's really important that you learn to greet Mrs. Wellington like a normal person. That means no growling, snarling, or hissing," Lulu explained calmly while seated in the classroom. "I've asked Theo to join us today to help with the demonstration."

Lulu then turned toward Theo, smiled, and waved. "Hey, Theo, how are you?"

"Lulu!" Theo screamed as he engulfed the girl in a mammoth hug. "I've missed you so much, *friend*!"

"Get off me," Lulu huffed, hard-heartedly pushing the boy away.

"Was that too much?"

"I said act *normal*. What part of that was *normal*?"

"I created a backstory to help me get into character. You've just been freed after twelve years as a prisoner in the Colombian jungle. So with that in mind, I would say my reaction was pretty normal," Theo explained.

"We are not practicing talk-show reunions; we're doing normal, everyday hellos," Lulu responded. "Do you understand? Or do I need to go over the definition of 'normal' again?"

"Actually, that could be really helpful. Sometimes it feels like English isn't my first language."

"Theo, you were born and raised in New York City."

"Or so my parents claim. I wouldn't be surprised if Joaquin kidnapped me from the streets of Canada as a young child."

"You do realize they speak English in Canada as well? And trust me, if Joaquin had kidnapped you, he would have returned you long ago."

"This is the thanks I get for rescuing you from the jungles of Colombia?" Theo said, shaking his head at Lulu.

"Oh, please, everyone knows you were thrown out of the Boy Scouts. The least you could have done is made up a believable backstory," Lulu railed at Theo as Abernathy looked on with confusion.

"I prefer the term 'dishonorably discharged,'" Theo huffed. "And that whole thing was blown way out of proportion."

"You hid food in your tent and almost got the whole troop mauled by a bear."

"Well, excuse me for wanting a midnight snack! And how was I supposed to know bears even liked hummus?"

"What was it you wanted me to do exactly?" Abernathy asked meekly as Theo and Lulu continued to argue, having momentarily forgotten the dire and terribly overwhelming predicament School of Fear was in.

CHAPTER 5

EVERYONE'S AFRAID OF SOMETHING:

Hypnophobia is the fear

of being hypnotized.

Days passed, lessons continued—and so did the relentless snooping of Sylvie Montgomery. On more than one occasion, Schmidty caught her swimming in the birdbath, hiding in the azalea bush, or posing as a statue outside the front door. To say the old man was peeved was an enormous understatement—he was downright livid. Not only was this woman determined to destroy his madame's career, she was stopping him from one of his greatest leisure activities: talking to himself. Schmidty had long enjoyed chatting about his daily stresses and concerns while minding the gardens. But of course with a reporter on the loose, this was no longer a possibility. So in an effort to deter Sylvie from hanging around the grounds, Schmidty had begun dousing her in Casu Frazigu. Unfortunately, it turned out Sylvie was rather fond of the specialty dish.

Sensing that time was fast running out and that Sylvie's tenacity would soon pay off, Schmidty decided to attempt hypnosis. After placing Mrs. Wellington on the drawing room couch, he dug out an old gold pocket watch. While the beautifully crafted family heirloom dated from 1803, it was hardly enough to keep Mrs. Wellington's attention. So Schmidty taped a picture of the old woman to the piece of jewelry, knowing nothing captured her interest quite like she did.

"Madame, please follow the picture with your eyes."

"As if I have a choice; I'm utterly ravishing! I literally can't keep my eyes off myself!"

"As always, your modesty amazes me," Schmidty said wryly as he continued to evenly swing the medallion. "Imagine you are walking down a staircase; picture each and every step."

"I thought you were hypnotizing me to stop loathing Abernathy. What's all this nonsense about stairs?"

"Madame, you and I both know you care very deeply for Abernathy."

"That boy has been a dark cloud over my life, haunting me, torturing my every second! And yet he's angry with me? What have I ever done to him, besides love his father?"

"Perhaps it's best we segue into the listening section — and just to be clear, *you* are expected to listen, not *me*."

"Is that your elaborate way of telling me to shut up?"

"Yes, Madame, it most certainly is," Schmidty said before prompting the woman to close her eyes and continue down the imaginary staircase.

Two floors down, Schmidty noticed a remarkable change in Mrs. Wellington's breathing.

"Madame," he whispered excitedly before hearing the definitive sound of a snore.

As Schmidty covered a slumbering Mrs. Wellington with a soft chenille blanket, Theo continued his tour de force makeover of Abernathy.

"A lot of people say you can wear pastel only near Easter, but I disagree," Theo said confidently as he led his student into the downstairs closet. "With your gray skin tone, soft colors will do wonders for you."

"And you're sure plaid and pastel go together?" Abernathy asked timidly.

"Plaid plus pastel plus fanny pack equals cool. End of discussion," Theo stated assuredly before breaking into some awkward stretches. "And as a special bonus, for today only, you are getting a one-on-one dance session with none other than Rumpmaster Funk."

"Let me guess—you're Rumpmaster Funk."

"That's right," Theo said as he broke into a movement that combined jumping jacks with a rogue hula hoop motion.

As Lulu, Theo, Madeleine, and Garrison worked tirelessly, time appeared to move at an accelerated speed. Soon Abernathy knew the names of all 192 United Nations member states, the starting lineup for the Yankees, and how to maintain eye contact. But most impressively, Abernathy had accomplished all of this while dressed in pastel and plaid. However, absolutely no progress was made where Mrs. Wellington was concerned. Abernathy still growled and snarled whenever she spoke to him.

After hearing of Schmidty's unsuccessful hypnosis session with Mrs. Wellington, Garrison decided to take the lead where Abernathy was concerned. He simply couldn't bear the idea of spending the rest of his life as a fraud, sending postcards from phony surfing holidays in Hawaii and Bali.

"You are falling into a deep trance," Garrison said to Abernathy, who was lying nearly horizontal in the dentist chair in the Fearnasium. "Your eyelids are growing heavier by the second. Soon, you will have no choice but to close them."

Lulled by Garrison's commanding voice, Abernathy quickly closed his eyes. At this point the tanned boy stared at the man's peaceful gray face and froze. Garrison simply hadn't a clue what to do next. "Um, we are currently experiencing technical difficulties. Please be patient, and we will be with you shortly."

"Technical difficulties?" Lulu surprised Garrison from behind. "This isn't the cable company; you can't just put him on hold."

"What are you doing here?"

"You didn't really think I was going to miss your first hypnosis session, did you?"

"It's a disaster! What am I supposed to say?"

Lulu winked at Garrison before bluntly asking what everyone was dying to know: "Abernathy, why do you hate Mrs. Wellington?"

The man's eyes fluttered rapidly beneath his eyelids, much as one might see in someone suffering a seizure.

"Maybe I shouldn't have asked that—what if it sends him into some sort of coma?"

"No way," Garrison muttered quietly in response. "That's ridiculous. You're starting to sound like Theo."

"I'll deny saying this if you ever tell him, but sometimes Theo is actually right. What if this is one of those times? What if I have accidentally caused our one and only hope of saving the school to have a seizure?"

As the color drained from Garrison's overly bronzed face, Abernathy slowly opened his chapped pink lips. Both Lulu and Garrison stared at him intently, frightened of what he'd do next.

"I had no choice; I promised her...."

"Promised who?" Lulu yelped excitedly—perhaps too excitedly, as it jolted the man.

"I need to go," Abernathy declared, opening his eyes and sitting straight up. Seconds later, he darted out of the Fearnasium without so much as a wave or look in Lulu and Garrison's direction.

"What do you think he meant when he said he had no choice?" Garrison repeated curiously to Lulu.

"I'm still wondering who *she* is...."

CHAPTER 6

EVERYONE'S AFRAID OF SOMETHING:

Dermatophobia is the fear

of skin lesions.

Failure is the most relentless of enemies, ravaging all who cross its path. And nowhere was this truer than with the School of Fearians. As their prospects of success dwindled, so did their confidence, inciting a marked regression in the students' behavior. And, try as they might, they simply couldn't resist sharing their rediscovered phobias with Abernathy.

"Spiders are essentially eight-legged criminals, dare I say terrorists, so if you see one, kill it. And that goes for insects as well. When in doubt, stomp first, ask questions later," Madeleine said politely while having afternoon tea with Abernathy in the classroom. "Another scone?"

"Madeleine," Abernathy chirped as he placed a scone on his small rose plate, "I spent a lot of time with spiders and insects while living in the forest."

"I hadn't thought of that. We really ought to bathe you in boric acid, just in case any creepy crawlers slipped in with you," Madeleine said as she pushed her chair away from Abernathy.

"Oh, no, I didn't mean to scare you. I promise no spiders or insects came in with me. I just wanted to tell you that they are actually pretty amazing creatures if you get to know them."

"Blasphemy!" Madeleine responded with such high drama that she could easily have been mistaken for Theo. "Abernathy, I loathe pulling rank, but I am the teacher, and that means I am *always* correct! SPIDERS MUST DIE!"

While Madeleine was focused on spiders and insects, Lulu returned to her unilateral distrust of elevators.

"How do we really know the doors are going to open

again? The government claims to monitor elevators, but with the economy tanking, something is bound to fall through the cracks. And my money is on elevator maintenance."

"But aren't there phones in elevators?" Abernathy asked quietly.

"I can't believe you even brought those up! They're less reliable than Theo on a diet!" Lulu shrieked, most illogically offended by Abernathy's comment.

Even Garrison, who was normally heralded for his cool façade, was starting to crumble in front of Abernathy.

"Surfing is all about being Zen, cool, and collected, and that's totally me," Garrison stated emphatically before his face started perspiring excessively. "My only problem with surfing is the water. Those currents will suck you out to sea and drown you slowly...."

Abernathy wondered why Garrison hadn't created a new persona based around rock climbing or hang gliding so that he could easily avoid water. But the boy was utterly disinterested in being anything other than a surfer, albeit a fraudulent one. However disturbing Abernathy's conversation with Garrison was, it paled in comparison to Theo's diatribe on danger. He literally listed seventeen ways to die within seventeen steps of the front door. After absorbing such macabre information, Abernathy was extraordinarily relieved to listen to Hyacinth sing—at least until he took note of the lyrics. The little girl had taken to singing about being alone and friendless after School of Fear closed.

With mere days left before Sylvie's article was to run, even Schmidty worried that School of Fear would soon find itself shuttered, forever disgraced. Following hours of nervous cooking and cleaning, the old man pondered his precarious future while lugging garbage to the back of Summerstone. Alone in the dark recesses of the yard, he fretted not for himself or even for Mrs. Wellington, but for the many fearful children in the world. Where would they go? Who would help them? His eyes clouded with tears as he opened the garbage bin and prepared to toss in the sack he held. Then something pink caught Schmidty's eye. Knowing of Mrs. Wellington's strict moratorium on throwing away anything pink, he instantly deduced that the blob must be Sylvie Montgomery.

"What are you doing in my trash?" Schmidty angrily asked the rosy-skinned reporter.

"Looking for leads," Sylvie said before snorting loudly, her nose aflame from all the secrets she sensed inside Schmidty.

"I'm afraid I'm going to have to ask you to leave the trash can, and the premises for that matter."

"You'll never be rid of me! I'm going to win the Snoopulitzer for this story! I can smell it already," Sylvie announced excitedly, holding up an imaginary award in her left hand. In the disgraceful, dishonest, and highly disreputable field of tabloid journalism, there was no higher honor than winning the Snoopulitzer.

By the following daybreak, Schmidty was electrified with concern over the escalating security breaches. With few options remaining, a grounds patrol was enacted. And while Hyacinth volunteered, she was immediately disqualified due to her incontrovertibly loquacious nature. It was, after all, her big mouth that had started the entire Sylvie Montgomery mess. As for Madeleine, she whole-heartedly refused to take part because of spiders' and insects' well-known proclivity for living outside. And

Garrison begged off after seeing some gray storm clouds overhead, concerned that a flash flood was on its way. This left only Theo and Lulu for the inaugural patrol of Summerstone's grounds.

"Must you eat like that?" Lulu asked as she watched Theo shove handfuls of dry cereal into his mouth before taking a swig of milk from the carton.

"We are on patrol; I need to be prepared to move at a second's notice. I can't be weighed down by a bowl and spoon. Honestly, Lulu, it's like you've never been on a stakeout before."

"This isn't a stakeout; we're basically mall cops."

"Do you take Visa? Because this doesn't look like the mall to me."

"You have the worst comebacks I have ever heard, and I do mean *ever.*"

"Excuse me," came a voice from behind Lulu and Theo, greatly surprising them. "I don't suppose you could help me? My name is Melissa, and I'm looking for School of Fear. I hear it really helps with . . . fears."

Standing before them, dressed in a blond wig braided into pigtails, a plaid school uniform, and thick glasses, was none other than Sylvie Montgomery. Try as she might to disguise herself, her nose and pink skin tone were unmistakable.

"Um, hello? Of course it's good with fears—that's why it's called School of *Fear*," Theo said condescendingly, clearly unaware of Melissa's true identity.

"You can't be serious," Lulu responded in disbelief.

"Please, I'm so scared. Won't you let me come inside?" Sylvie asked impatiently.

"What exactly is it that you're afraid of, *Melissa*?" Lulu asked through gritted teeth.

Sylvie suddenly froze, caught completely off guard by the question. She opened her mouth, then closed her mouth, then opened it again and blurted out, "Mangoes."

"Mangoes?" Theo repeated. "I guess that hairy seed could be kind of creepy."

"Theo, it's Sylvie Montgomery! The pink face? The nose? The weird body? Please tell me you knew it was her."

"Um, of course, Lulu," Theo blustered. "I was just undercover a second ago."

"As who?"

"I was undercover as myself, or more precisely a version of myself that didn't know that Melissa was really

Sylvie," Theo said before turning toward the nosy reporter. "How dare you come around here causing all these problems? This is School of Fear, and in case you haven't figured it out by now, we have enough problems already!"

"Can I quote you on that?" Sylvie asked with exhilaration.

"He's a minor; you can't quote him without parental permission," Lulu said, slapping her hand over Theo's mouth.

"Quite the legal mind," Sylvie responded, sniffing loudly. "I'll give you anything you want for the inside scoop."

"You want the inside scoop? I think you have allergies. It's not normal for a nose to make so much noise," Lulu shot back.

"What about you, kid?" Sylvie asked Theo with a wink.

"I think there's also a very good chance that you're suffering from rosacea; your skin shouldn't be that pink."

"This is no time for jokes; you have no idea who you're messing with!"

"Who's joking? Your skin is screaming for a good dermatologist!"

"In that case, perhaps I can get Dr. Bregman's number from you?"

"How do you know my dermatologist's name?" Theo asked nervously.

"I know all your doctors' names, and your teachers', and your neighbors'," Sylvie said with another snort. "I know just about everything there is to know about you guys."

"Yeah, right," Lulu replied halfheartedly.

"You stole the key to the teachers' restroom just so you could use a bathroom with a window," Sylvie said matter-of-factly.

"How could you know that?" Lulu asked, shocked.

"Like I said, I know absolutely everything about you kids," Sylvie said confidently. "And as for those last few secrets about your teacher and the school, I'll sniff them out soon enough...."

CHAPTER 7

EVERYONE'S AFRAID OF SOMETHING:

Aviophobia is the fear

of flying.

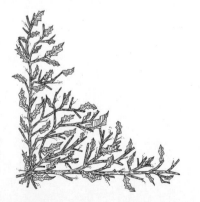

As the outcome of her contestants' plan grew dimmer, Mrs. Wellington retreated to her bed in the middle of the day. With a bleak forecast for the remainder of her life, she hardly had a reason to stay awake. And so as Lulu and Theo finished their first patrol, the old woman fell quickly and quietly to sleep in her oversized pink bed.

Upon waking from her nap a few hours later, Mrs. Wellington trotted to the mirror to reapply her makeup and brush out her wig. The old woman looked at her reflection and realized she must still be asleep. There was simply no other explanation for what she saw. Mrs. Wellington promptly pinched herself, only to find that she was in fact conscious. She immediately began to rub her eyes, absolutely sure that dust particles were distorting her vision. After thirty seconds of diligent massaging, Mrs. Wellington once again looked in the mirror. Still the inexplicable image persisted, which could only mean one thing: it was real.

"I'll kill him!" Mrs. Wellington erupted as she stormed down the stairs, through the foyer, and into the Great Hall.

Alarmed by the commotion, Schmidty, Abernathy, and the students rushed into the corridor from the classroom. There stood Mrs. Wellington, sporting a massacred wig, a literal mess of short jagged spikes.

"Man, that is one bad haircut," Garrison muttered as he surveyed the damage.

"I think it's kind of punk rock," Lulu said optimistically. "If you add some leather and chains to your wardrobe, you can totally pull this off."

"You ruined my last wig," Mrs. Wellington spat venomously at a smiling Abernathy.

"Mister Abernathy, I beg of you to stop smirking. It's hardly helping the situation," Schmidty pleaded while nervously wringing his hands.

"Well, you ruined my life, you shrew!" Abernathy retaliated loudly.

"Celery wants to know what a shrew is," Hyacinth said in her usual peppy voice. "I totally know, but you know how ferrets can be...."

"Hyacinth," Lulu said with a sigh.

"Hyhy," Hyacinth corrected her.

"Tell Celery to get a dictionary because we don't have time for this!" Lulu huffed.

"You're pure evil," Abernathy bellowed at Mrs. Wellington before once again beginning to growl and snarl.

"You ruined my hair! That's tantamount to treason where I come from," Mrs. Wellington declared before breaking into a guttural hiss.

"Ugh, not the animal-kingdom thing again," Garrison said with frustration.

Fortunately, the animalesque brawl was interrupted

by Summerstone's seldom-heard doorbell. In a nod to Mrs. Wellington's pageant history, the bell played the Miss America theme song, not that anyone other than Schmidty and Mrs. Wellington recognized it.

"Old man, open this door," Mrs. Wellington ordered Schmidty after stomping into the foyer with all but Abernathy in tow.

"Yes, of course, Madame."

Standing on the doorstep in a Girl Scout uniform was the ubiquitous Sylvie Montgomery. Dressed in an emerald skirt with socks pulled up to her knees and a sash covered in badges, Sylvie looked disturbingly authentic. One couldn't help but wonder if a local Girl Scout would soon discover her uniform missing from the clothesline.

"Hi, I'm Jenny! Would you like to buy some Girl Scout Cookies?" Sylvie said from beneath a thick layer of white makeup, a desperate attempt to camouflage her Pepto-Bismol skin tone.

"Finally, something goes my way. We'll take twelve boxes of Thin Mints and all the Samoas you've got," Theo stated euphorically.

"Again, Theo?" Lulu asked, shaking her head in disbelief.

"You really can't tell it's Sylvie?" Garrison asked with a most perplexed expression.

"Dear Mister Theo, for the country's sake, may you never work in espionage," Schmidty added.

Sylvie took one small step toward the door, desperately angling her head to get a better view of Garrison.

"Well, if it isn't the boy who offered to teach Ashley Minnelli how to surf even though he can barely swim," Sylvie said excitedly, staring at Garrison.

"How do you know about that?" Garrison exploded as Madeleine simultaneously screamed, "Who is Ashley Minnelli?"

"Leave the students out of this!" Mrs. Wellington snapped ferociously at Sylvie.

"It's a little late for that. I'm including all their weird and embarrassing secrets in the article. It will make the story all the more compelling to the Snoopulitzer committee," Sylvie announced proudly as Mrs. Wellington slammed the door.

"I guess that means no cookies," Theo lamented sadly.

The group stood still, silently taking stock of their extraordinarily grim predicament. With only days left before the story went to press, they were faced with a few undeniable truths: Abernathy still loathed Mrs. Wellington, and Sylvie's passion for the story was increasing exponentially by the day. Unless they stopped her, she would publicly humiliate them all, literally exposing their deepest, darkest secrets to the world.

"We failed you," Garrison announced glumly to Mrs. Wellington and Schmidty.

"He's right," Lulu agreed. "It's over. Well, except for the part where she tells the world all of our horrifying secrets, which should make the first day back at school a real treat."

"At least you're young," Mrs. Wellington said quietly. "There's still time to change your names and build new lives. For me, this is it."

"I can't believe this is happening. I thought School of Fear was too big to fail, sort of like all those companies on Wall Street," Theo moaned morosely.

"As acting academic tutor of the house," Madeleine explained, "I feel it is my duty to inform you that many companies on Wall Street did in fact fail."

"Oh, no, I wonder if my uncle lost his job. Although on the bright side, if he did, at least I'll have someone to hang out with while I'm being homeschooled. There's no way I'm showing my face at school after the article," Theo blustered.

"Ashley Minnelli is going to find out that I'm not a surfer, that I can't even watch *SpongeBob SquarePants* without getting a sweaty upper lip," Garrison groaned.

"Oh, enough about Ashley!" Madeleine snapped most uncharacteristically. "Sorry, I don't know what's gotten into me; it must be the stress. I'm sure Ashley is a lovely girl, absolutely lovely. And best of all, she probably doesn't wear a shower cap."

As Madeleine looked at her feet, her cheeks burning bright red, Garrison turned away, unsure what to say or do to make it better.

"It's not over yet," Schmidty said, nervously patting his comb-over.

"I think your hearing aid needs the volume turned up; we just covered how we totally and completely failed," Garrison corrected the old man.

"Well, there's still one option left...."

"Oh, come on, Schmidty!" Theo yelled. "We don't have time for dramatic pauses!"

"I was merely pausing to breathe, Mister Theo, and I

hardly think you are in a position to lecture anyone where drama is concerned," Schmidty huffed before turning to Mrs. Wellington and whispering in her ear.

"Hey!" Lulu barked. "We don't have time for secrets, either!"

Mrs. Wellington's eyes flitted about the room nervously as she contemplated what Schmidty had said.

"Oh, dear, you aren't going to sell us to Munchauser, are you?" Madeleine asked quietly, silently reminiscing about Mrs. Wellington's grotesque, gambling-obsessed attorney.

"Why would you even plant that idea in their heads?" Theo responded disapprovingly.

"Please, Schmidty, won't you tell us what you're thinking?" Madeleine asked nicely.

"Madame, it's your call. You know him better than I do."

Mrs. Wellington's eyes again flitted around the room, as if she were frantically searching for the right answer, before landing on Schmidty. After a few seconds the old woman cautiously nodded her head in agreement.

"The man's name is Basmati...."

CHAPTER 8

EVERYONE'S AFRAID OF SOMETHING:

Hobophobia is the fear

of bums or beggars.

Bishop Basmati is the most contrary man in the world. If you say 'black,' he will most definitely say 'white.' And if you then say 'white' he will deny he ever said 'white.' He simply cannot agree with anyone. So contrary and tricky is Basmati that simply being in his presence rids children of difficult behavior," Mrs. Wellington explained to her rapt students.

"He runs the Contrary Conservatory in upstate New

York," Schmidty added. "Along with School of Fear, it's one of the few specialty institutions left in the country."

"Well, what are we waiting for?" Garrison asked. "Let's go see this guy."

"I think it's best if we stop and call Basmati so he has time to go grocery shopping before our arrival," Theo added seriously. "As I always say, an empty cupboard leads to an empty brain. And I think we can all agree, if we've ever needed full brains, it's now."

"I'm beginning to question if you even have a brain," Lulu said to Theo.

"I'm afraid the Contrary Conservatory abides by the same no-technology stance as we do," Schmidty explained. "So this will have to be a surprise visit, snacks and all."

Never in the history of Summerstone had anyone packed as fast as Abernathy. The man simply placed his toothbrush in his fanny pack and considered himself ready. After years of forest living he felt that changing his clothes more than two times a month was most extravagant. Mrs. Wellington, on the other hand, found it impossible to leave Summerstone without a minimum of ten outfits, a backup case of makeup, and her infamous pageant tutu. So obscene was her amount of clothing for the short trip that the students and Schmidty actually had to aid her in packing.

After finally wrangling the eight-person, two-animal group out the front door, Schmidty shot the flare gun, signaling for the sheriff to come to the base of the mountain. Unfortunately, as the sheriff was attending to actual city business, issuing a jaywalking ticket to an elderly man, the group was forced to wait almost twenty minutes. Standing next to the Summerstone Vertical Tram, the eclectic group watched flying squirrels glide effortlessly from branch to branch along the perimeter of the Lost Forest.

"Do you ever miss the forest?" Lulu whispered quietly to Abernathy.

"Not like I thought I would," Abernathy replied, clearly surprised by his own response. "There are a lot of nice people out here. Well, except for her," he added with a nod at Mrs. Wellington.

Upon arriving at the base of Summerstone, the sheriff agreed to drive the group to Pittsfield Airport, therefore removing the greatest danger from the trip: Mrs. Wellington behind the wheel. The memory of the horrifying drive to the Pageant for Pooches was still clearly etched in everyone's mind, as was Mrs. Wellington's subsequent arrest.

While none of the children had an explicit fear of flying, Lulu and Theo were definitely uneasy with the idea. For her part, Lulu was extremely worried about being trapped in midair, literally marooned in the sky, without any possible means of escape. Theo, on the other hand, was deeply concerned about everything that happened between takeoff and landing—the plane, the pilot, the peanuts.

Pittsfield Airport was the sort of small-town establishment that crafted signs using paper and felt-tip pens. Constructed out of a converted auto-body garage, it had questionable security to say the least; upon entering, the group was faced with a handwritten note that asked all passengers carrying illegal weapons or other forms of contraband to please turn around and drive to Boston's Logan Airport.

"I am officially naming the plane Besties Airway!" Hyacinth cheered as she ran toward one of the two gates at the airport.

"Um, no way," Lulu said with her hand firmly covering her twitching left eye. "That is not a plane; that is a coffin with wings. And quite frankly I don't think Theo could fit in there even if he was wearing a girdle."

"How do you know about my girdle?" Theo asked anxiously before getting distracted by the rusted blue plane with lopsided wings and cracked windows.

"Let's just rent a car and take our chances with Mrs. Wellington," Lulu declared boldly.

"I have to agree with Lulu on this. That thing is a death trap. It doesn't even have proper wheels, just a couple of Rollerblades glued to the bottom," Theo exclaimed nervously.

"Chubby, I cannot believe that you and Macaroni are actually wearing parachutes," Mrs. Wellington said, pointing to the canvas sacks strapped to their backs.

"Scoff all you want to, but these are the wave of the future," Theo retorted. "And PS, don't you think there's a reason they sell them at the gift shop? And by gift shop I mean the homeless man standing by the front door."

"Theo, Lulu," Madeleine said calmly, "why don't I ask the pilot to come out here and answer all your questions? That's sure to put you at ease."

Madeleine walked straight onto the tarmac, where

she sweetly waved for the pilot of the rusted blue mound to come hither. And though she believed it was her kind face that lured the pilot from the cockpit, it was something else entirely: his curiosity about her shower cap.

Pilot Aronson, a tall and commanding man in his forties, immediately sensed something was amiss upon meeting Lulu and Theo. Of course, it *was* rather hard to ignore Theo's Lamaze breathing or Lulu's nervous twisting of her hair.

"I understand you kids have some questions," Pilot Aronson said to the School of Fearians.

"I prefer to be called an adult or, at least, an adult-in-training," Theo said haughtily. "Now for my first question: Has this plane passed the 60716554AD56GFC7 inspection?"

"I've been a pilot for twenty years, and I've never heard of that."

"Good," Theo said, nodding his head. "That was a trick question. There is no such thing as the 60716554AD56GFC7 inspection."

"What's the square footage on that thing?" Lulu asked while obsessively licking her lips in reaction to her suddenly dry mouth.

"About two hundred fifty square feet."

"So about the size of a coffin or a French elevator or another comparable death trap," Lulu muttered, her face white with fear.

"Even though you appear to know what you're doing, Pilot Aronson, the bulldog and I will still be wearing parachutes as a precaution," Theo announced before turning to Lulu. *"As a Precaution* is another great potential title for my memoir."

"Stop talking about your memoir. You haven't even gone through puberty yet!"

"I'll have you know that just this morning I saw a hair on my chin," Theo retorted as Lulu rolled her eyes. "Okay, fine, it was one of Macaroni's hairs that just happened to blow onto my face. But if that's not foreshadowing, what is?"

"Sorry to interrupt, but do you guys have any other questions for me?" Pilot Aronson asked with exasperation.

"Does your flight attendant know CPR?" Theo asked dramatically, raising his eyebrows.

"My flight attendant's name is Maggie, and yes, she is certified in first aid, including CPR," Pilot Aronson responded reassuringly.

"Okay, good, but I hope she isn't the overeager type because I'm saving my first kiss for someone special, if you know what I mean," Theo said.

"He doesn't know what you mean. No one knows what you mean. I don't even think you know what you mean!" Lulu blurted out.

After all the questions were asked and answered, Garrison and Madeleine boarded the plane, followed by Mrs. Wellington, Hyacinth, Abernathy, and Schmidty. Lulu and Theo remained parked on the tarmac, staring up at the rusted mess of metal.

"I don't think I can do it. It's so small," Lulu said as her voice began to quiver.

"But there are windows, Lulu," Theo said reassuringly. "And you love windows. There are even cracks in some of them, so you'll have fresh air."

"No, it's too tiny."

"It's bigger than our bathroom, and you've spent more than forty-five minutes in there, so what's the big deal?"

Lulu looked at Theo sweetly and smiled. "Just when I thought you were an idiot, you had to go and make sense. Come on, let's do this."

"Nah, you go ahead. Mac and I are going to sit this one out."

"What about the great pep talk you just gave me?"

"It *was* pretty good, wasn't it?"

"Get on the plane, Fatty! We need you!"

"But Lulu, it already looks like it's been in a crash! That is *not* a good sign!"

"Theo, you're a hall monitor," Lulu said, feigning seriousness. "Either rise to the occasion or I'm going to have to turn you in to the Board of Ethical Hall Monitors and have your sash revoked."

Gasping in horror, Theo unfolded his sash and slipped it onto his body while sucking in his belly. Outside of eating, being a hall monitor was Theo's greatest joy in life, and he had no intention of giving it up.

"Let's do this!" the boy yelled bravely before performing one of his famous Rumpmaster Funk dance moves.

"Hold that thought," Lulu muttered as she watched two airport workers struggle to load a large and unusually bulky white canvas sack onto the back of the plane. "Remember that story you told me about the man who hid an alligator in his luggage?"

"Do you think Hyacinth put an alligator in her bag to get back at me for calling Celery a racist?"

"What? You called the ferret a racist?"

"She hates me because I'm fat."

"For the last time, fat people are not a race!"

"Alligators love fatties; we'll be dead by takeoff," Theo mumbled to Macaroni as Lulu sprinted toward the back of the plane.

CHAPTER 9

EVERYONE'S AFRAID OF SOMETHING:

Herpetophopia is the fear

of reptiles.

In reality, there wasn't an alligator on the plane, but a pig. Stuffed into the large canvas sack was none other than Sylvie Montgomery. The story of the man hiding an alligator had merely given Lulu the idea of a stowaway, and sure enough, she was right. The feisty girl had the baggage handlers remove the wiggling white sack, inside of which the perturbed reporter grunted loudly.

"You can still save yourself, Lulu. Give me the goods on your teacher and I won't run any of your secrets—

109

not even the one about you shoplifting at the country club."

"I wasn't shoplifting! They sold me damaged merchandise then refused to give me my money back! I was merely righting a wrong!"

"I doubt your parents will see it in that light," Sylvie said as she inhaled loudly through her snout.

"Hey, guys," Lulu called out to the nearby baggage handlers. "This is trash. Just toss it in the Dumpster!"

After the encounter with Sylvie, Lulu was so angry and preoccupied that she was able to board the plane without incident. Only once the door closed behind her did she begin to hyperventilate from the low ceiling and narrow breadth of the space. After Lulu made a quick escape attempt, Theo and Garrison literally pinned her to her seat while the plane left the ground. Her lungs tightened and her body convulsed with fear. She was trapped. Short of jumping to her death, there was no way out.

After almost ten minutes of straining against both Theo and Garrison, she relaxed. Just as a doctor had once told her, the human body can sustain panic for only so long. Though she was still frightened and shaky, the urge to throw herself out the door had subsided.

Once Theo was free of focusing on Lulu, his own anxiety over the journey returned ferociously. His eyes literally bulged at the sight of exposed wires crawling dangerously along the plane's walls.

"I really hope these chutes were packed properly. As it is, Mac's going to have trouble pulling the string without an opposable thumb," Theo babbled anxiously.

"I wouldn't worry; the flight is going to be over in a flash," Madeleine said calmly. "And on the bright side, Mrs. Wellington just informed me that all spiders and insects die above ten thousand feet. Isn't that spectacular?"

Lulu and Garrison immediately turned to Mrs. Wellington, both recognizing that she had lied to Madeleine about elevation killing insects. The old woman merely winked in response.

"Are they going to pass out peanuts soon?" Theo asked while nervously tapping his fingers on his armrest. "I'm starving, and so is Mac!"

"Celery and I are deathly allergic to peanuts, so we

would appreciate it if, as a bestie, you would refrain from consuming all peanut products. After all, you wouldn't want to accidentally kill us."

"No, we certainly wouldn't want it to be an *accident,*" Lulu remarked with a smirk.

"Don't worry, Hyacinth, Lulu's been threatening to kill me since I met her, and I'm still alive," Theo said. "Although who knows for how long, since I'm currently on a plane held together by Scotch tape."

"Hey there, passengers," said Maggie, the saucy brunette flight attendant, upon exiting the cockpit in a snug navy uniform. "I don't want to alarm anyone, but—"

"Then don't," Theo interrupted forcefully. "I can't handle much more! I just saw a piece of the wing break off!"

"Oh, I wouldn't worry about that. Wings are the tonsils of aviation; no one really needs them," Maggie explained. "But there is something else...."

However, as fate would have it, before Maggie could inform the passengers of the problem, the plane abruptly descended in a nosedive. So steep and sudden was the drop that all the passengers experienced momentary whiplash, including Macaroni and Celery. As the plane

112

plummeted toward the ground, panic-stricken screams filled the chamber. Yet, even amid the rampant shrieking, one voice set itself apart.

"I don't want to die!" Abernathy wailed. "My life is just beginning! I finally have friends who aren't insects!"

Much like a roller coaster, the plane suddenly leveled out before beginning an almost vertical ascent. As the passengers caught their breath, Maggie stood up and attempted to regain her bearings.

"Everyone please remain calm. We are not going to die. Or at least it's unlikely we're going to die. Of course, I can't say it's totally impossible," Maggie blathered uneasily.

"Those are not very reassuring words," Mrs. Wellington snapped. "As a forty-nine-time pageant winner, I demand to know what's happening!"

"It's the alligator, isn't it?" Theo asked, hysterically weeping. "The alligator ate the pilot! There's no one flying the plane!"

"Just tell us what's happening!" Garrison screamed at Maggie as the plane tilted from side to side.

"We have reason to believe there's a person in the engine who's interfering with the plane's ability to fly properly."

"What's your reason?" Garrison asked impatiently.

"We can see her head popping out from time to time. It's pretty hot in there, so she's probably trying to cool down. Unfortunately, every time she moves she hits wires and cylinders, causing the plane to move erratically."

"What kind of airline are you running here? You let people ride in the engine?" Mrs. Wellington warbled angrily. "I demand a refund!"

"Should we actually survive, I'm open to discussing that," Maggie said tensely to Mrs. Wellington, only to be answered by the sound of a ferret vomiting.

"Sorry, ferrets are really sensitive to motion. That's why you rarely see them at amusement parks," Hyacinth explained, holding the ferret's small head in a barf bag.

"Oh, that's why I never see ferrets at Disneyland," Lulu said with a sarcastic sneer as the plane vibrated violently.

"I'm confused; are we dying or not?" Abernathy squealed in an abnormally high-pitched tone.

"Why? Are you ready to make peace with me?" Mrs. Wellington asked, her face contorting with optimism.

Abernathy responded by looking directly at Mrs. Wellington without either snarling or growling for the first time. With this one simple act, the mood in the plane shifted toward hope and possibility.

"We're most likely *not* dying," Maggie answered. "Pilot Aronson is trying to land the plane without killing us or the stowaway. And the good news is, we're hoping to crash close to the airfield."

"That passes for good news? Pathetic," Theo mumbled while performing a multitude of religious hand gestures. Sadly, he wasn't sure what half of them meant, or—worse—if he had made them up.

"Am I correct in assuming that the person in the engine has the complexion of bubblegum?" Schmidty asked while diligently holding his comb-over in place; he had a most terrible fear of dying with bad hair.

"How did you know?" Maggie shrieked as the plane once again fell into a steep nosedive.

"Would you ask the pilot to try to crash in an area without any visible signs of bugs or spiders?" Madeleine yelled at Maggie before continuing her silent prayer for survival.

A sound like that of a chain saw cutting through a radiator reverberated as the whole craft pulsated uncontrollably. As instructed by Maggie, the passengers quickly tightened their seat belts and braced for impact. With her life flashing before her eyes, Maggie, a recently ordained Internet minister, prepared to offer last rites. However, before she could even open her mouth, the plane came to a thunderous halt in a clearing.

"Is everyone okay?" Mrs. Wellington asked the group before turning to make direct eye contact with her stepson. "Abernathy?"

All the signs of promise that had been displayed only moments earlier evaporated as Abernathy viciously snarled and growled at Mrs. Wellington.

"I bet you crashed this plane on purpose to try to make me forgive you!"

"I did not," Mrs. Wellington snapped. "What kind of lunatic do you take me for?"

"The kind who would fake her own death!"

"Who told him that?" Mrs. Wellington demanded angrily of the children.

Hyacinth nodded in Theo's direction as the boy all but climbed beneath Macaroni's bulky body.

"Madame, Mister Abernathy," Schmidty said sternly, "might we continue this altercation outside?"

Just then a loud and most disturbing snorting sound

came from the front of the plane and resonated through the chamber. As Pilot Aronson opened the cockpit door, the group saw a flash of Sylvie through the windshield. Rather spectacularly, she was unharmed, aside from minimal bruising.

"Did someone forget to mention that a crazy woman who looks like a pig is stalking them?" Pilot Aronson asked animatedly.

"Yes, now that I think about it, I *did* forget to mention Sylvie," Mrs. Wellington said without a tinge of embarrassment. "I can tell you now if you like: there's a crazy woman who looks like a pig stalking me."

"How do we plan to get out of here without Sylvie on our tail?" Garrison asked.

"Pilot Aronson, how far are we from the airport?" Lulu inquired, covering her throbbing left eye.

"We're here."

"But this is just a dirt field," Madeleine said, looking out the window.

"Welcome to Sarnacville Airport, also known as a dirt field," Pilot Aronson announced before returning to the cockpit to radio for help.

"Oh, no, look at all those trees! I bet they're loaded

with creepy crawlers absolutely desperate to torment me," Madeleine screeched, panicky.

"But why would they want to torment you?" Abernathy squeaked reasonably.

"How should I know? You're the one who's friends with them," Madeleine barked aggressively, or as aggressively as a polite English girl is capable of.

Pilot Aronson quickly returned to the cabin with an important update.

"The pig lady's foot is stuck in the fan belt, so if you're looking to make a break for it, now would be a good time."

"I've decided it most prudent that I remain on the plane," Madeleine stated quietly.

"Madeleine wants to stay on the plane, I think she is insane, something's wrong with her brain, let's order chow mein," Hyacinth sang inappropriately.

"That sounds like a Top 40 hit to me," Abernathy said sweetly.

"Insect lover," Madeleine grumbled at Abernathy. "I don't care what anyone says; I shall remain here."

"I didn't want to have to tell you this, but Mrs. Wellington's whole spiders-die-at-ten-thousand-feet thing is nonsense. And if you don't believe me, there's a huge web behind you to prove it," Lulu explained seriously to Madeleine.

"How could you?" Madeleine hollered at Mrs. Wellington as she leaped for the door.

Mrs. Wellington quickly surveyed the plane and noted that there wasn't a web in sight.

"Don't be so surprised. You're not the only one who knows how to lie for someone else's own good," Lulu said with a smirk.

"Well done, contestant. Although I prefer the term 'fib'; it's less likely to be used against you in a court of law," Mrs. Wellington said as she exited onto the dusty field.

While Sylvie Montgomery could not actually see the group departing the plane, she could definitely smell them. Her spherical snout was sniffing with unbridled intensity as each member marched off the busted mess of metal.

"You won't escape!" Sylvie screamed, still firmly lodged in the engine. "My nose will find you! You're only making my story all the more worthy of a Snoopulitzer!"

With Mrs. Wellington and Schmidty in the lead, the group stealthily tiptoed to the edge of the clearing and into a dense cluster of trees. Flowering crab apple and thick-trunked maples beguiled the madcap mob as they rushed down a barely discernible path.

"Do you guys know where you're going? Because after a plane crash, getting lost in the woods is not high on my wish list," Lulu groaned to Mrs. Wellington and Schmidty.

"Of course we know where we're going. We've been here more times than a cat can count," Mrs. Wellington stated, pushing pink-blossomed branches out of her way.

"Do you hear that? It sounds like flying water beetles or mutant airborne spiders," Madeleine fretted feverishly as she attempted to pull her shower cap over her entire body.

"Uh-oh, I think the Brit's going batty again," Theo assessed rather impolitely.

"Maddie," Garrison said reassuringly, "Lulu, Theo, and I are going to create a human shield to make sure no insects or spiders can get within three feet of you."

"Thank you," Madeleine whimpered as the three-some surrounded her, swatting away every last gnat, spider, and bug.

Following closely behind the human bug repellers were Hyacinth, Celery, Macaroni, and Abernathy. While Macaroni usually preferred the company of Theo, he found all the arm-waving more than a tad bothersome. Oddly, he didn't mind the tone-deaf Christmas carols Hyacinth and Abernathy belted out, proof that canine hearing may not be as superior as previously thought.

"Is anyone else starting to hate Santa?" Lulu asked, clearly annoyed by Hyacinth and Abernathy's rendition of "Santa Says Smile."

"I'm boycotting the whole month of December," Garrison grunted.

"Who cares about Santa? Aren't you guys worried about this Basmati fellow? I'm barely able to handle Mrs. Wellington, and now we're meeting another off-the-grid teacher. For all we know, this guy just escaped from the mental ward at Guantánamo Bay," Theo whispered frantically to Lulu, Madeleine, and Garrison.

"Is that the pirate ride at Disneyland?" Garrison asked earnestly.

Madeleine blushed as she looked at Garrison. As gorgeous and kind as he was, he really hadn't a clue about the world.

"Garrison, Guantánamo Bay is a detainment facility in Cuba, built to hold prisoners from Afghanistan and Iraq," Madeleine offered with a kind smile.

"Thanks, Maddie. I don't know what I'd do without you."

Upon hearing this, Madeleine turned a shade of red she didn't even know existed. She was simultaneously excited, embarrassed, and electrified by his comment.

"Theo has a point about Basmati. We haven't a clue what we're getting into with him. For all we know, he could make the Abernathy situation worse," Madeleine said, flinching at the sight of a bee twenty feet away.

"You say that as if it could possibly get worse! In case you haven't noticed, we are at rock bottom. Sylvie is about to destroy the school and publicly humiliate us all in one fell swoop," Lulu stated firmly.

"Wrong," Garrison replied authoritatively. "Where Wellington is concerned . . . it can always get worse."

CHAPTER 10

EVERYONE'S AFRAID OF SOMETHING:

Asthenophobia is the fear

of fainting.

W hat is that?" Lulu griped as she plugged her nose. "Theo, did you pass gas?"

"How dare you?" Theo thundered. "I would never! Well, at least not in the presence of other people. What do you take me for, a bulldog?"

"That's not Theo," Madeleine quickly assessed. "Sulfur dioxide smells like rotten eggs. My guess is there are hot springs nearby."

"Hot springs? How much water are we talking about?

125

A bucket? A bathtub? A pool?" Garrison asked with escalating concern.

"Contestants! Hurry!" Mrs. Wellington called out from around the bend.

As Lulu, Madeleine, Garrison, Theo, Hyacinth, and Abernathy turned the corner, gray clouds ominously passed overhead. With the last shred of sunlight fading, the group took in their new surroundings. It was a strange and unique union of beauty and peril. Barbed wire rambled across the stone wall like a wild unkempt vine, its jagged points shimmering in the setting sun.

Surrounding the spherical fortress wall was a moat with clouds of sulfur lingering just above the surface. Weathered by years of steam, the narrow wooden draw-bridge was held precariously together by frayed twine and rusted nails. So absorbed was the group by their new environment, they unanimously failed to notice Garrison's drastic change in demeanor.

Within the span of two minutes Garrison had begun to sweat so profusely that his hair was drenched and his clothes were visibly damp. The mere thought of crossing the moat via the flimsy bridge had sent the boy into a downward spiral of panic and perspiration.

126

Madeleine, the first to notice Garrison's predicament, sweetly placed her hand on his moist arm, saying, "Garrison, are you all right? You look a bit peaked."

"I feel so hot and light-headed," Garrison answered, his eyes bouncing around like pinballs.

"I think someone's about to pass out," Lulu muttered as the sweaty boy swayed from side to side.

And sure enough, that's exactly what happened; seconds later, Garrison collapsed into a wet ball atop the grass.

"I've never seen Madeleine move that fast for *me*," Theo complained loudly as the shower cap–clad girl ran to Garrison's side.

"Mister Theo," Schmidty reprimanded, "I think it best for you to keep such thoughts to yourself."

"Everyone needs to focus!" Mrs. Wellington hollered while pulling at her matching periwinkle skirt and top. "We need to get across so we can pull up the drawbridge before Sylvie finds us. With that nasty nose, she could be here any second!"

Upon hearing Mrs. Wellington's voice, Abernathy broke into a rather disturbing roar. Even Macaroni and Celery appeared frightened by the mammalian sound of aggression. Perhaps decades alone with wild animals was simply too much to overcome? But just as the group began to look at him differently, Abernathy delivered one of his clumsy insults, instantly removing all fear from the equation.

"You're uglier than this place smells," Abernathy ineptly derided Mrs. Wellington.

"Man, you're bad at talking trash," Garrison uttered softly as he opened his eyes.

"Are you all right?" Madeleine inquired, hunching protectively over the weary boy.

"Gary! I tried to grab you, but you went down so fast," Theo said to Garrison.

"That's a total lie! You didn't even move," Lulu scolded Theo.

"My mind wanted to help; it just didn't have a chance to tell my body."

"Celery wants to know why your mind lets your body wear pastel and plaid together," Hyacinth said to Theo.

Abernathy, dressed in an outfit nearly identical to Theo's, looked downright shocked by Hyacinth's comment. He had been led to believe that pastel on plaid was the height of fashion, especially when paired with a fanny pack.

"At least I wear clothes. Celery walks around stark naked. I'm surprised she hasn't been arrested for public indecency," Theo shot back spitefully.

"Enough! There must be total silence when Schmidty tests the bridge. If it collapses, dumping him straight into a boiling pot of piranhas, I want to hear his final words. Of course, knowing Schmidty, they'll probably be rather boring," Mrs. Wellington said with a sigh.

"Piranhas in a hot spring? I don't think so," Lulu scoffed.

"I wouldn't be so sure; Basmati used to keep a pack of piranhas in every toilet in his house," Mrs. Wellington explained before turning to Schmidty. "What are you waiting for? Hop to it! But please don't *actually* hop; your jiggling stomach is most unattractive."

"As is your personality, Madame. Oh, and thank you for yet another opportunity to act as your personal lab rat. I'm most obliged," Schmidty said wryly as he stepped onto the dwindling drawbridge.

The rotund man wobbled and hobbled across the

uneven wood, straining his eyes with each step. It was not so much the precarious nature of the lumber that worried Schmidty, but his own vision. If he didn't pay close attention he was liable to step right off the narrow walkway.

As Abernathy, Madeleine, Lulu, Hyacinth, Garrison, Theo, and Mrs. Wellington held their breath in anticipation, a troubling noise captured their attention. It was the familiar sound of Sylvie's snorting. Alarmed, all but Madeleine and Garrison rushed onto the bridge, causing it to sag perilously beneath their feet.

Having caught a glimpse of pink dashing through the nearby trees, Madeleine forcefully grabbed Garrison's hand. While normally too shy for such an act, she hadn't time to ponder her behavior with Sylvie in dogged pursuit.

"Garrison, you need to come with me across the bridge," Madeleine pleaded impatiently. "I promise it will be over before you know it!"

"Go without me," Garrison muttered, his eyes flitting about uneasily.

"But Sylvie's coming!"

"Don't worry, I won't tell her anything."

"No, Garrison! That is unacceptable. You are the de facto leader and as such cannot act like a pansy! Now, move!" Madeleine ordered him.

"What does 'de facto' mean? Wait—did you just call me a pansy?" Garrison asked as Sylvie ran breathlessly toward them. Lucky for the School of Fearians, much like an actual pig, Sylvie lacked endurance where physical exercise was concerned.

"I said move it, *PANSY*!" Madeleine screamed ferociously, doing her best impression of an angry coach goading a player from the side of the field.

So unnerved was Garrison by Madeleine's conduct that he did in fact start moving. He stepped onto the rickety bridge, innately aware that only a few flimsy pieces of wood stood between him and his mortal enemy, water.

"Faster, Feldman," Madeleine bellowed. "This isn't the bench! You need to move it, Feldman! She's almost here!"

Now only ten feet away was a visibly bruised Sylvie, her normally pink nose crimson from excessive sniffing.

"You'll never escape me," Sylvie squealed victoriously as she daringly leaped for the rising drawbridge.

Fortunately, they all made it across, and Schmidty was able to harness his considerable body mass to successfully lift the drawbridge within a hair of Sylvie stepping on it. As the others helped the old man tie up the wooden walkway, Garrison collapsed onto the ground next to Madeleine.

"Do you really think I'm a pansy?"

"Of course not," Madeleine replied honestly. "But I had to get you to cross that bridge, didn't I?"

"Thanks, Maddie, you've always got my back," Garrison said before sweetly throwing his arm around her shoulders, causing the petite girl to absolutely melt with euphoria.

Once the group was safely inside the fortress, a slew of contradictory signs greeted them: NO TRESPASSING, TRESPASS AT YOUR LEISURE, GET OUT, COME IN, ENTER KINDLY, EXIT ANGRILY. All in all, it was a terribly perplexing welcome.

The Contrary Conservatory's residence was most bizarre and awfully difficult to describe. It was an amalgamation of several architectural styles crudely blended together. Bits of Gothic castles, igloos, and tree houses stuck out every which way without any decipherable rhyme or reason. Diverse elements such as limestone towers, artificial ice blocks, and rope swings combined to create an extraordinary eyesore.

Similar to the residence, the Contrary Conservatory's grounds were an interesting assortment of landscapes, ranging from a Japanese sand garden to a cacti cluster to brilliantly sculpted topiaries and much more.

"Contestants," Mrs. Wellington said as she attempted to straighten the monstrous mess that was her wig, "Bishop Basmati can be rather odd, so it's best to follow my lead. Unless, of course, my lead isn't working, in which case try something else."

"Madame, your advice is as ineffective and useless as ever," Schmidty muttered under his breath.

As Mrs. Wellington reapplied thick mauve lipstick, a strange rattle started overhead. Madeleine was the first to spot the shoddily built metal go-cart flying off a slanted igloo section of the roof. Much like the plane they had only just escaped, the cart was precariously held together by twine and tape. Jagged pieces of multi-colored metal flew off the basic wooden frame as the cart became airborne. Even though they were standing at least fifteen feet away, the School of Fearians all shielded themselves from the flying scraps of tin.

The go-cart's poorly constructed frame crumbled instantly upon touching the earth, quickly burying its passengers beneath debris. Within seconds, Schmidty and Abernathy rushed over to help. However, before they could grab even one piece of wood from the pile, three teenage boys surfaced from the rubble covered in an impressive array of bumps and bruises. Instead of tears or pained expressions, the boys displayed unbridled ecstasy; they had clearly crashed *on purpose.*

"That was awesome!" a stout redheaded teenager declared while pumping his fist in the air.

"You must be this summer's Contrarians. I assume you're all okay, as you're standing and don't appear to be hemorrhaging," Mrs. Wellington stated disapprovingly.

"Theo Bartholomew at your service," Theo said, extending his hand to the ginger-haired boy, who most unfortunately had the body of a tree trunk and the face of a pancake. "I'd like to check you for signs of internal bleeding, concussions, and mental illness because, let's be honest, you just drove off the roof—that's pretty crazy."

"Have you ever jumped off a hundred-foot cliff?" the flat-faced boy asked Theo.

"What? Of course not; that's why I'm still alive," Theo replied as he struggled to grasp the direction of the conversation.

"Did I ever tell you about the time I broke my brother's arm with my mouth?"

"I just met you six seconds ago; I don't even know your name."

"Fitzy Flint. And this is Bard Bates and Herman Hester," Fitzy said, motioning to the two skinny brown-haired boys behind him. Bard and Herman were utterly indistinguishable in all ways but one: Bard moved incessantly, never standing still for more than a second. Even if he was simply tapping his foot or bopping his head, the boy was in constant motion. Herman, on the other hand, remained eerily still, almost catatonic, between activities.

"Nice to meet you guys. Let me introduce—" Theo said as he turned toward his fellow School of Fearians.

"Do you guys like to light stuff on fire?" Fitzy interrupted excitedly.

"Yeah! Fire!" Bard and Herman simultaneously grunted from beneath their coffee-colored mounds of hair.

"If you don't mind my inquiring, where are you guys from?" Madeleine asked while suspiciously inspecting the three boys.

"California," Fitzy answered, and Bard and Herman nodded their heads in agreement.

"Well, that explains a lot. Celery says people from California are crazy, like totally certifiable," Hyacinth chirped with the ferret seated comfortably atop her left shoulder.

"We mustn't generalize about groups of people. Although it would be disingenuous to say I haven't heard the same," Madeleine responded while keeping her eyes peeled for creepy-crawly life-forms.

"Do you guys want to see if Bard's hair is flammable?"

"Are you bonkers? Of course it is," Madeleine snapped before shaking her head judgmentally at Fitzy.

"We won't know for sure until we try," Fitzy countered firmly. "We thought my mouth was flammable, but it turns out it isn't."

"You tried to light your mouth on fire?" Garrison repeated in disbelief.

"Yeah, after I drank some hair spray."

"That could kill you!" Theo screeched, flailing his hands about theatrically.

"No way," Fitzy said before pumping his fist in the air and screaming. "Fire!"

As if answering a call of duty, the Contrarians bolted across the yard. While intellectually challenged and deficient in common sense, they were clearly quite physically adept.

"Well, that was weird," Theo stated. "But on a positive note, I'm grateful to have Joaquin as a brother for the first time in my life."

"What, he's never broken your arm with his mouth?" Lulu asked sarcastically.

"Not successfully. But more important, he doesn't play with fire, drink hair spray, or combine the two activities."

"I must say I'm quite appreciative to be an only child at this moment," Madeleine offered frankly.

"Me, too," Garrison agreed.

As usual, Madeleine blushed, absolutely delighted to have something in common with Garrison.

"Do you smell smoke?" Lulu asked the others.

"It appears Bard, Herman, and Fitzy have lit a potted plant on fire," Madeleine said, motioning toward the far end of the yard.

"I suppose it's preferable to lighting Bard's hair on fire," Mrs. Wellington offered matter-of-factly.

"Should we get a fire extinguisher or the hose?" Theo sensibly wondered aloud.

"I don't think that will be necessary," Schmidty said as he watched the boys kick the flaming plant into a small fountain.

"I already have a bad feeling about this place, and we haven't even met Basmati yet," Theo whimpered as they approached the vaulted front door to the Contrary Conservatory.

CHAPTER 11

EVERYONE'S AFRAID OF SOMETHING:

Ornithophobia is the fear

of birds.

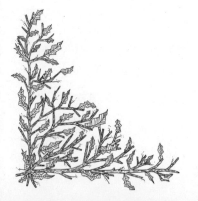

G O AWAY TOMORROW, COME BACK YESTERDAY was
the motto carved ornately into the front door of
the Contrary Conservatory. Paying the message no
mind, Mrs. Wellington vigorously clanged the copper
bell to announce her arrival. As they waited for an
answer, a tremendous and unexpected sense of failure
took hold of her. For all her success as a teacher, she had
failed the student who mattered most: her stepson. Suddenly teary-eyed, the old woman distracted herself by

smoothing imaginary wrinkles on her periwinkle skirt. There simply wasn't time for such emotional indulgence. Basmati was the last line of defense, and Mrs. Wellington needed to be as strong as possible to deal with him.

After banishing all tear-inducing thoughts from her mind, Mrs. Wellington assumed her customary pageant pose. With her back arched, her right knee bent, and her left hand on her hip, Mrs. Wellington reminded herself that once a beauty queen, always a beauty queen. Tough times and a butchered wig were no excuse for abandoning the basic tenets of pageantry. And so, as the door swung open, she greeted Basmati with a friendly Vaseline-coated smile and a mechanical wave.

Mrs. Wellington and Schmidty had known Basmati for years and as such were fully prepared for the vision that greeted them. The same could not be said for Abernathy and the students, who stood awestruck at the sight of him. The middle-aged man of average weight and average height was anything but average. Much like the Contrary Conservatory itself, Basmati's blond hair was a mishmash of styles. Long curly locks descended from the left side of his scalp, while the right remained inexplicably bald. His coarse handlebar mustache solely inhabited the right facial sphere, while his lone eyebrow took the left. The entire look was topped off with a tee shirt that read I MARRIED A LIMA BEAN on the front and I DIVORCED A LIMA BEAN on the back.

"Edith Wellington, I'd know you *anywhere*! Well, maybe not *there,* but definitely *here,*" Basmati muttered with an accent best described as Daffy Duck by way of Jerusalem, Shanghai, and Berlin.

"Bishop Basmati," Mrs. Wellington replied genially. "I'm sorry to arrive without proper notice, but I am in desperate need of your help."

"Why didn't you say so?"

"I thought I just did," Mrs. Wellington replied logically.

"Just did what?" Basmati asked, curiously raising his sole eyebrow.

"I just told you I need your help."

"But I don't need your help."

"Yes, I know that...."

"What do you know?" Basmati questioned a now visibly frustrated Mrs. Wellington.

"I know that I need your help, but that you don't need mine."

"I didn't know you needed my help; you should have mentioned something sooner."

"Yes, of course, you're absolutely right," Mrs. Wellington relented, giving in to the utter madness that was Basmati.

"Liar! You already told me that you needed my help!" Basmati responded forcefully while attempting to slam the large wooden door shut.

In a move that clearly demonstrated her desperation, Mrs. Wellington shoved her head into the fast-closing space between the door and its frame.

"Please! If my stepson, Abernathy, doesn't forgive me in the next three days, I'll lose everything. Well, except my looks, that is," Mrs. Wellington pleaded feverishly with her head still jammed in the doorway. "Won't you at least let me in so we can discuss this?"

"Let you in where?" Basmati asked, opening the door happily.

"No wonder you never married. Speaking to you is exhausting!"

"May I offer you some coffee then?" Basmati said kindly, almost normally.

"Oh, that would be lovely," Mrs. Wellington said with a fatigued sigh.

"What would be lovely?" Basmati asked with a suddenly blank expression.

"Coffee would be lovely."

"I detest coffee. I've never had a sip in my life! If you were really my friend, you would never have uttered that word in my presence," Basmati screamed irrationally at Mrs. Wellington, shocking the students and Abernathy.

"In that case, I'll leave," Mrs. Wellington bluffed.

"Edith Wellington and company, won't you please come in?" Basmati asked politely, motioning for the group to enter his eccentric residence.

The interior of the Contrary Conservatory could only be described as schizophrenic. So diverse and bizarre was the space that it nearly defied explanation. Immediately upon entering, the group was met with two large bronze statues: an elephant and a donkey. However, these were not just any old elephant and donkey; these were rivals, the mascots for the Republican and Democratic parties. Once past the animals, the children noticed the writing on the wall, quite literally. The empty room's floor had been stenciled with the message, THIS IS THE CEILING, while the ceiling stated, THIS IS THE FLOOR, and—perhaps most bizarrely—the walls stated, I AM BOTH THE CEILING AND THE FLOOR, THEY ARE BUT MERE IMPOSTORS.

The group exited the room via a fourteen-foot metal tunnel guarded by two solid-gold figurines of a tortoise and a hare. Madeleine lagged behind to stare at the statues, utterly gobsmacked by the sight of such opulence at the Contrary Conservatory. She also couldn't help wondering about the worth of such items in light of the recent increase in the price of gold.

"Forget it, Maddie, they're too heavy; we'll never be able to get them out of here," Lulu joked as she grabbed Madeleine's arm and pulled her into the tunnel.

The dark, damp, and dreadfully dreary passageway fed directly into a room known as the Hospital for Spreading Contagious Diseases.

"This is the first institute of its kind, a place built solely to aid healthy people in getting sick," Basmati explained proudly as Theo ran ahead, desperate to exit the germ-ridden facility.

"Celery doesn't get it—why would anyone want to get sick?" Hyacinth asked Basmati.

"So they can get better! There is nothing better than feeling well after being sick. But of course you can't feel better if you never felt sick...."

Following the Hospital for Spreading Contagious Diseases were the Racetrack for Snails, the Atheist's Church, the Court of Lawlessness, and finally the Standing-Room-Only Sitting Room.

"Won't you please have a seat?" Basmati asked graciously as they entered, seemingly oblivious to the state of the room.

The moderately sized space was filled with a grand leather sofa, two matching wing chairs, and a large mahogany coffee table, only they were all overturned, with their legs facing the ceiling.

"I think we'll stand," Schmidty replied, surveying the furniture.

"Am I to understand that you are taking a stand against sitting in the Standing-Room-Only Sitting Room?" Basmati inquired irritably of Schmidty.

"Let's hang back here," Garrison whispered to

Abernathy, Lulu, Hyacinth, and Madeleine. "Probably best not to get too close to this guy."

Theo, on the other hand, charged full speed ahead, squeezing in between Schmidty, Mrs. Wellington, and Basmati.

"I hate to be nosy—actually, that's not true; I've always enjoyed being a bit of an amateur sleuth. Anyway, bottom line: Did you really marry a lima bean?" Theo asked curiously, pondering the legality of a legume nuptial.

"Mister Theo," Schmidty interrupted, "I implore you to use some common sense, or at the very least think before you speak."

Ignoring Schmidty, Basmati stepped closer to Theo, bent down and positioned himself mere inches from the boy's face, and whispered, "Did you marry a lima bean?"

"No way! I don't even like lima beans. I could see myself with a french fry or grilled cheese sandwich, maybe, but never a lima bean," Theo replied most illogically.

"How dare you talk about my wife that way?" Basmati bellowed angrily into the boy's round face.

"So you *did* marry a lima bean?" Theo replied with the zeal of Sherlock Holmes solving his first case.

"Absolutely not! Everyone knows lima beans are gold diggers!"

"Oh, enough about lima beans!" Mrs. Wellington hollered. "I need your help with my stepson! Please, Basmati!"

"Is the boy married to a lima bean your stepson?" Basmati asked, motioning to Theo.

"I already told you, I didn't marry a lima bean! I'm not even old enough to get married," Theo huffed under his breath.

"No, Theo is not my stepson. Although I'm flattered you think I'm young enough to have one his age. I knew that do-it-yourself face-lift would work," Mrs. Wellington said with a satisfied smile before turning solemnly toward Abernathy. "No, my stepson is that man over there."

The simple act of Mrs. Wellington pointing at Abernathy elicited an irate grunt from the man. Standing between Hyacinth, Madeleine, and Garrison, Abernathy exposed his teeth, narrowed his eyes, and emitted brutish animal sounds. The ferocity of the noise instantly depressed Mrs. Wellington, causing a pathetic frown to take hold of her face.

After explaining her terribly dire predicament to Basmati, Mrs. Wellington pursed her lips and prayed the man would agree to help.

"We're a dying breed, Edith Wellington. The need for schools such as ours remains, yet we continue to disappear," Basmati said sadly. "I wish I could help. I honestly do, but I have a much bigger problem. They've stolen Toothpaste...."

"We can buy you more toothpaste," Mrs. Wellington declared assuredly.

"Toothpaste is my canary. He's the only one in the world who disagrees with everything I say. And you know how much I need that. Every morning I wake excited to say 'hello,' only for him to respond 'goodbye.' But now Toothpaste's gone. They came in the middle of the night and took him."

"He named his canary Toothpaste," Hyacinth scoffed quietly to Lulu.

"You named your ferret Celery; you're hardly in a position to judge," Lulu whispered before turning to catch an engrossed Theo grabbing Basmati by the arm.

"Who took him? The Mafia? The CIA? The FBI? The Bermuda Triangle?" Theo questioned Basmati absurdly, instantly intrigued by the animal abduction.

"No, my students—Fitzy, Bard, and Herman! They didn't like my lessons, so they stole the one thing I care about. Toothpaste is my sole weakness. They've promised not to hurt him as long as I let them do whatever they want. I even gave them matches."

"But what if they eat him? I mean, Fitzy drinks hair spray. I wouldn't even be surprised if he had eaten his own arm in the womb. If you know what I mean," Theo babbled.

"Celery doesn't know what you mean," Hyacinth said as she and the others crept closer.

"Neither do I," Lulu seconded, "but it sounds gross."

"I think it's something to do with Fitzy having eaten his own flesh," Madeleine said with a look of disgust. "Honestly, Theo, such a comment is highly distasteful, even for you."

"I didn't mean Fitzy *actually* ate his arm. I just meant he and his cronies seem weird. I wouldn't put a little bird barbecue past them."

"I think I understand," Basmati said grimly as he

looked into Theo's brown eyes. "You know something, don't you? Did you help them? Did you kill my bird? You did, didn't you? You're a bird killer!"

"No! I'm a vegetarian! I love animals. They're my best friends! Just ask Macaroni! Actually, he doesn't speak English. But if he did, he would tell you I love animals!"

"You hate animals! It's written all over your face," Basmati answered Theo.

"What? No! That's just my natural expression. I swear," Theo replied nervously. "Did I mention I volunteer at a squirrel-cide hotline? I talk suicidal squirrels off the ledge. Would an animal hater do that?"

"Chunk, get a grip," Lulu muttered quietly to Theo.

"Okay, maybe I made that last part up, but I really do love animals. I would never hurt Toothpaste. As a matter of fact, I'm not leaving here until I rescue him. Toothpaste is the Lindbergh baby of our generation!"

"That is a dreadful analogy, Theo. The Lindbergh baby died," Madeleine explained morbidly.

"Fine, then he's our Patty Hearst!"

"Who's Patty Hearst?" Garrison asked.

"Patty Hearst is an heiress who was kidnapped,

brainwashed, and forced to take part in a bank robbery. She subsequently went to prison but was eventually freed and pardoned. Now, while Patty lived, I must disagree with this analogy as well. I highly doubt Toothpaste is being brainwashed and trained for larceny."

"Would you stop with the historical facts? The important thing is that my inner activist is back! Free Toothpaste! Free Toothpaste! Free Toothpaste! Free Toothpaste!" Theo chanted animatedly.

"Chubby, have you completely forgotten about saving School of Fear? We don't have time to rescue Toothpaste! We need to rescue ourselves," Mrs. Wellington snapped in disbelief.

Basmati gazed intently at the School of Fearians, looking each and every one of them over before closing his eyes. After a few seconds, he opened his eyes and began humming rather loudly. This was a most unusual sort of humming, as it was fast-paced and frenetic in style, almost operatic. The School of Fearians watched with perplexed expressions as Basmati then began conducting himself, waving his arms rapidly back and forth as his humming reached a crescendo.

"He's actually pretty good; I would totally hire him

for a party or bar mitzvah or something," Theo mumbled to Madeleine as the odd man finished.

Mrs. Wellington watched Basmati closely, unsure how to interpret his musical interlude. After all, it certainly wasn't every day that a man broke into a humming opera in the middle of a conversation. But for Basmati, humming was a means of clearing his mind before making an important decision.

"If you promise to bring back Toothpaste, I'll handle your stepson," Basmati announced unemotionally while staring at Mrs. Wellington.

The old woman turned and assessed Theo, Lulu, Garrison, Madeleine, and Hyacinth. They were the strongest students she had ever had, and as such she trusted them implicitly.

"I give you my word: we will find Toothpaste and bring him home."

CHAPTER 12

EVERYONE'S AFRAID OF SOMETHING:

Ophidiophobia is the fear

of snakes.

The sleeping arrangements at the Contrary Conservatory proved exceptionally limited due to the high number of guests and peculiar use of space. Much like the first floor, the second floor had a bevy of bizarre rooms, such as the Greenhouse for Dead Plants, the Brightly Lit Dark Room, and the Reverse Tanning Booth for Turning People Pale. However, nowhere in the entire residence was there a single bedroom. As he had his whole life, Basmati slept in a bathtub, considering cold porcelain to be the height of comfort. With this in mind, it was hardly a surprise that he had sent the Contrarians to sleep on the old wooden pews in the Atheist's Church.

After much hemming and hawing, Basmati finally decided upon the School of Fearians' sleeping quarters. He placed Mrs. Wellington in the Greenhouse for Dead Plants, Abernathy and Schmidty in the attic, and the children in the basement. His logic was as follows: Mrs. Wellington was so old she could go at any second, and if she did in fact die, the greenhouse would be the perfect place to store her body. As for Schmidty and Abernathy, the attic possibly contained a bunk bed suitable for the duo, but most important, there was little of value up there to break. (Basmati was concerned that Schmidty's portly frame could do damage to some of the house's more delicate items.) Lastly, Basmati offered the children the choice of either the Hospital for Spreading Contagious Diseases or the basement, two rooms he deemed capable of handling the wear and tear of children and animals. Rather understandably, as no one was interested in contracting a contagious disease, the children thought the basement a better bet.

After bidding good night to the others, Mrs. Wellington made her way to the greenhouse. The glass-encased room, filled with hot, dry air, was designed to literally dehydrate plants to death. Overflowing with mounds of brown foliage and dried flowers, the dreary space did not contain one stick of furniture. So, after lying on the hard floor and finding herself unable to sleep, Mrs. Wellington grabbed a few dead plants to use as cushions. And while the slight pricks of the thorns did not bother her, the incessant crinkling drove her mad. The noise conjured up images of Macaroni gobbling kibble, saliva spraying everywhere. As much as Mrs. Wellington loved Macaroni, she loathed the sound of him eating.

Situated directly next to the greenhouse was a copper-plated elevator on the verge of dilapidation. This was the sole means of accessing the attic. Fatigued after a long's day journey, Schmidty and Abernathy halfheartedly shoved their bodies into the narrow cart and closed the cagelike door. While the elevator sputtered toward the attic, Schmidty's tremendous polyester-clad stomach pressed awkwardly against Abernathy's side. It was a most unfortunate scenario, as Schmidty was nearly as sensitive about his stomach as he was about his combover. Regardless of what he told Theo, he too was ashamed of his protruding midsection. For this reason, he had long pulled his black slacks up to his armpits, desperate to create an optical illusion.

Eager to escape the close confines of the elevator, both Schmidty and Abernathy darted out upon reaching the attic, where they were greeted by an impenetrable wall of debris. Broken furniture, boxes, and much more created a daunting obstacle between them and the bunk beds they'd been more or less promised. (Basmati had confirmed and refuted the existence of the bed more times than either Schmidty or Abernathy could count.)

"This reminds me of when you were a boy, and I would search the grounds of Summerstone for you," said Schmidty to Abernathy. "Sometimes it took hours to track you down, but when I did, you always smiled, and then I couldn't stay mad at you. Do you remember those days?"

"Of course. You were always so kind to me...not like *her*," Abernathy squeaked, digging through the rubble of the attic.

"Oh, it wasn't all bad with Madame; don't you remember when she took you to the circus? You were so fond of that monkey—what was his name?"

"Garfunkle. And I wasn't fond of him, Schmidty, I was handcuffed to him."

"Yes, now that you mention it, that does sound familiar. Of course, Madame was only trying to stop you from running away. She knew you wouldn't get far with a monkey on your arm."

"Schmidty, do you recall how that night ended?"

"With ice cream sundaes in the kitchen?"

"Garfunkle tried to kiss me!"

"Perhaps this wasn't the best memory to bring up, although in Garfunkle's defense, you had spent the whole night together; he might have thought it was a date."

"I don't blame Garfunkle, I blame *her*. She's the one who stole my father and ruined everything," Abernathy muttered in a most resentful and childlike manner.

"You seem to forget that your father fell in love with Madame as much as she did with him...." Schmidty trailed off as he ineffectively tried to move a large brown box from his path.

At that moment Abernathy was grateful to be hidden between an old dresser and a trash bag full of clothes. Pain contorted his face as he processed Schmidty's words. The same alarming, yet logical, thought had slipped into his mind many times over the years. And on each occasion, Abernathy found it too agonizing to even entertain. He had built his life upon the premise that his father was good and his stepmother was bad, and he had no intention of reevaluating the notion now.

"I found it!" Abernathy called out, slowly advancing toward the child-sized bunk beds with linens dating from World War II.

"Excellent, Mister Abernathy. I shall be there in twelve to fifteen minutes," Schmidty said as he assessed the mountain of wreckage separating the two of them.

With his body throbbing from mental and physical exhaustion, Abernathy collapsed onto the bottom bunk. Spending time with his stepmother, surviving a plane crash, and confronting his worst fear about his father made for a terribly overwhelming day. As a matter of fact, by the time Schmidty finally found the beds, Abernathy was fast asleep. Regrettably, this meant Schmidty had to take the top bunk, a most dangerous scenario for all involved.

While Schmidty attempted to sleep, his portly frame bowing mere inches above Abernathy, the students made their way to their subterranean sleeping quarters. The basement's walls were lined with splintered wooden slats, rusted pipes, and clusters of wild brown and white mushrooms.

"My throat feels funny. I think some of these mushrooms could be poisonous," Theo whimpered, frightened, as he looked at the walls.

"Are you sure it's the mushrooms?" Garrison asked skeptically. "Because I don't feel anything, and I'm breathing the same air you are."

"I almost died from eating a moldy mushroom once, so excuse me if I'm a little sensitive!"

"Why would you ever eat a moldy mushroom?" Garrison asked incredulously.

"I thought it was blue cheese... and I love blue cheese."

"Celery doesn't think anyone should eat moldy food, unless of course they're homeless and have no choice. Sadly, homelessness is a big problem in the ferret community. Ever since the economy tanked people have been leaving their ferrets to fend for themselves. And they can't just Dumpster-dive like cats and dogs do; ferrets are total food snobs."

"I don't have time to worry about homeless ferrets!"

Theo lamented dramatically. "What if toxic mushroom spores stunt my development? I'm counting on a significant growth spurt to spread out my chunk!"

"Theo," Madeleine said firmly, "I assure you, mushroom spores will not harm you. Your fears are wholly unfounded, scientifically speaking, so please calm down."

"Thank you Maddie," Theo blustered as he caught his breath.

"Now on to more pressing issues. As I'm sure you're aware, basements are well known hideouts for spiders, especially black widows," Madeleine said as she surveyed the shadowy corners of the room.

"Don't worry, Maddie, we'll be fine on the ground," Garrison said feebly, once again looking over their dreary accommodations. "Of course, we're sleeping under rusted pipes that could burst at any second, possibly drowning us to death in the basement of the Contrary Conservatory. But other than that there's nothing to worry about...."

"The floor is a creepy-crawly highway, and I have absolutely no intention of putting my body in the middle of it!" Madeleine exploded, clinging hysterically to her shower cap. "I'm just going to have to sleep standing up."

"That's physically impossible," Theo replied, shaking his head knowingly. "My late cat Barney tried to do it at least twice a day, and he never lasted more than a second."

"With all due respect for your deceased cat Barney, if a flamingo can do it, so can I!" Madeleine announced decisively.

"This is going to be so fun! Our first bestie sleepover in a basement!" Hyacinth said elatedly.

"It looks more like a dungeon than a basement to me," Lulu said as her chest tightened and her left eye tickled with tension. She didn't want to sleep in a windowless room, especially one below ground level. Panic pulsed through her body until she suddenly remembered the harrowing plane ride earlier that afternoon. Having survived such a thing had given Lulu an odd sensation, one of confidence in her abilities. If she could handle a plane the size of a bathroom, she could spend one night in a basement.

All in all, though, it was a dreadfully fitful night for the School of Fearians. For in addition to the dingy locale, they also had to contend with Macaroni's snoring and Celery's chirping. It is a little-known fact that ferrets, like humans, often talk in their sleep. So it was hardly a surprise that the students awoke with bloodshot eyes and tortured expressions. Basmati, on the other hand, rose contentedly, with an extraordinary sense of purpose. Not since the abduction of Toothpaste had he bounded out of bed so quickly.

After combing his half a mustache and half a head of hair and smoothing his one eyebrow, Basmati eagerly attended to Abernathy. Dressed in a flamboyant red sequined jacket, a nun's wimple, a tartan kilt, and sensible white nurse's shoes, Basmati led Mrs. Wellington's stepson to the Court of Lawlessness. Seated at the judge's bench, Basmati pulled two saltine crackers and a can of whipped cream from his jacket. Most curiously, he considered this to be a perfectly well-balanced breakfast.

As Abernathy quietly chewed the last of his cracker and cream, Basmati lifted his eyebrow and cleared his throat.

"Abernathy, I've been informed that you detest your stepmother, Edith Wellington," Basmati said, speaking with the calm focus of a prosecutor questioning a defendant.

"I despise the woman with every fiber of my being,"

Abernathy screeched harshly while wiping the remnants of whipped cream from his gray cheek.

"Murder is hard to forgive," Basmati replied casually, rubbing the bald half of his head.

"She killed someone?" Abernathy blurted out, utterly astonished by this new information.

"Of course she did! Edith Wellington killed you — or haven't you heard? That's why you're so furious with her; you're dead. Dead people are always angry. But who can blame them? They're dead!"

"I admit that I'm a really confused man, but I'm pretty sure I'm alive."

"Ohhhhh, I see," Basmati said, nodding his head to convey his understanding. "You may want to look into some blusher or bronzer; your gray skin tone can be misleading."

Abernathy looked uncomfortably around at the highly polished wooden walls of the courtroom, unsure how to respond to the suggestion of makeup.

"So you're alive, and you hate your stepmother for sending you to prison or, as I like to call it, the big house with bars and really cold metal toilets," Basmati surmised, pursing his lips.

"What? I've never been to prison! I've never even gotten a parking ticket! I have no idea where you are getting these ideas from. The truth is very simple: I hate *her* because she stole my father from me," Abernathy clarified loudly.

"Mrs. Wellington kidnapped him? I didn't think she had it in her. Petty larceny, sure, but a felony?"

"She didn't kidnap him. She did something much worse: she married him."

Again Basmati nodded excessively to demonstrate his understanding. After a minimum of thirty-four quick bobs, he began maniacally twirling his one-sided mustache.

"And after the wedding, Edith Wellington cheated on your father with an extraterrestrial?" Basmati proclaimed with astonishment. "If I hadn't heard it directly from your mouth, I wouldn't have believed it! What shocking behavior! Not for the extraterrestrial, but for Edith. Everyone knows aliens play fast and loose with their morals, but beauty queens? Never!"

"This is insane; I never said she had an affair with an alien," Abernathy exclaimed matter-of-factly.

"Of course you did! And there is absolutely no reason to deny it; who wouldn't be angry if their stepmother cheated on their father with a lesser species? It's completely logical," Basmati countered in a frighteningly resolute manner.

"That is not why I hate her! Why won't you listen to me? It's because she married him!"

"Don't be silly! You could never be *this mad* at her just because she loved him; it must have something to do with her affair with the alien. It's the only logical explanation. Well, that or the fact that she ran off with your fiancée the llama."

"I may have spent most of my life in a forest, but I have never been engaged to a llama!"

"Oh, I'm sorry; it was an alpaca, wasn't it? I always get those two confused."

"Please listen to me: I have never been engaged to an animal! Sure, I talked to them a lot while living in the forest, but that's as far as it went!" Abernathy spat out seriously before standing and making his way to the door.

"This is a court of law without laws, which means you can leave whenever you want to. However, I should tell you it is still considered rude to walk away without so much as a kiss on the cheek, a wave, or simply a goodbye!"

"Sorry," Abernathy muttered. "Goodbye."

"I don't know what that alpaca saw in him," Basmati mumbled as the door clanged shut.

CHAPTER 13

EVERYONE'S AFRAID OF SOMETHING:

Apotemnophobia is the fear

of people with amputations.

In light of the enormous time restrictions before Sylvie's story was to go to press, the School of Fearians immediately began their mission to save Toothpaste. They started with a search of the premises, looking in every cupboard, closet, and chest for the small but chatty bird. After two hours, however, having neither heard a peep nor found a feather, they all agreed it was unlikely the bird had been stashed inside.

"Okay, the bird's not here, or at least not anywhere

we can see, so I think it's time we formulate some kind of plan," Garrison said to the others, huddled in the middle of the Standing-Room-Only Sitting Room.

"Does stopping to have a snack count as a plan?" Theo asked earnestly.

"No!" Lulu answered decisively. "Feeding your tapeworm is just going to have to wait."

"That was uncalled for! You know darn well tapeworms come from eating meat! Are you implying I'm a covert carnivore? A fraudulent vegetarian?"

"Would everyone please stop talking about tapeworms? Just the thought of one makes me feel rather green," Madeleine said, steadying herself against the wall.

"Totally, Mad Mad," Hyacinth agreed. "Plus, Celery suffered a pretty traumatic loss last year when her bestie Arthur, a ground worm, was murdered by a crow right in front of her eyes. She had nightmares for, like, a week.... It was super intense."

"A week? That's it? Some friend," Theo muttered under his breath.

"Celery says you're in no position to judge, seeing as you once mourned the loss of a sandwich for, like, a month."

"They discontinued the ultimate veggie western burger! It was a major milestone in my life! And for the record, it was three and a half weeks, not a month."

"Enough about worms and sandwiches," Garrison said with a frustrated sigh. "We need to find this bird so we can get out of here. I don't know about you guys, but I really don't want to spend another night in that basement."

"We could do bird calls around the yard and see if Toothpaste responds," Madeleine suggested halfheartedly.

"Are you expecting the canary to call out, 'Hey, guys, I'm over here'?" Lulu asked skeptically.

"No, but I thought he might just fly to us if he heard his name."

"I'm pretty sure they're keeping him in some sort of confined space, seeing as they *kidnapped* him," Lulu responded patronizingly.

"Well, what do you suggest, Lulu?" Madeleine pushed back.

"Why don't we just ask them? They seem pretty dumb; they'll probably tell us."

"Sounds good to me," Theo said as he smoothed his hall-monitor sash. "I am ready when you are."

"Actually, I bet these guys will respond to Garrison and me better. You know, 'cause we're cool and stuff," Lulu stated confidently.

"Celery thinks you have a pretty big ego, which, like a big butt, isn't so attractive," said Hyacinth.

Theo and Madeleine couldn't help but smile; never had they so agreed with anything Celery said.

Shortly thereafter, Lulu and Garrison descended upon the extensive mishmash of gardens in search of the Contrarians. Considering the boys' fondness for fire, they half expected to find them by following a trail of flames. However, they soon discovered that absolutely nothing was smoking, smoldering, or burning, leaving them very little to go on. As a matter of fact, it wasn't until the two leaned against a soaring elm tree to strategize that they received a sign from above, quite literally.

"I say we hit the cacti cluster. They're probably removing the needles to perform satanic rituals on one another," Lulu surmised sarcastically while twirling a lock of her long strawberry blond hair.

"We just need to keep our eyes peeled — somewhere, something is on fire," Garrison said in response.

"Let's just hope it's not Toothpaste."

At that moment a most unusual stick fell from the sky and bonked Lulu directly on the head. Red and curly, it was the most peculiar twig she had ever seen. Of course, that's because it was actually a snake. And while Lulu wasn't afraid of snakes, she didn't like the idea of them falling from the sky.

"Hey, can you guys grab Bard's pet snake, Petey? He's really attached to him," Fitzy called out from the second-highest branch of the towering tree.

Bard, who was pacing frantically on the branch, screamed, "Petey," as if he were calling after a wayward dog.

Garrison stared at the motionless red snake and realized something wasn't quite right. It hadn't moved, not even a centimeter, since falling from the tree. Memories of Mrs. Wellington's taxidermied horses swept through his mind, offering a sudden flash of clarity.

"You stuffed your snake?" Garrison said in disbelief as he picked the stiff creature up off the ground.

"Bard says dead pets make the best pets. You don't

have to feed them or walk them or clean out their cages. You just have to remember to stuff them; otherwise they turn all black and moldy. Really, the only hard part is finding a dead one," Fitzy rambled.

"Speaking of pets," Lulu said nicely, looking up at the three boys, who appeared to be rigging some sort of dubious contraption. "Where's the bird?"

"Want to bungee jump? It's really fun," Fitzy responded eagerly, totally ignoring Lulu's question.

"As tempting as that sounds, I'm going to have to pass," Lulu replied. "But as I was saying, where's the bird?"

"What bird?" Fitzy answered distractedly.

"You know what bird," Lulu shot back.

"Big Bird? Toucan Sam? I don't think I know any other birds. Wait, is Tinker Bell a bird? She flies and has wings, but she doesn't have a beak," Fitzy pondered seriously.

"We're talking about Toothpaste the canary!" Garrison exploded. "Where is he?"

"Toothpaste! Man, I almost forgot about him," Fitzy said, shaking his head. "That little dude sure can talk."

"Where is he?" Lulu pressed on impatiently. "Just tell us where you stashed Toothpaste!"

"Why does Basmati call him Toothpaste? It's such a stupid name. Dental Floss would be way cooler," Fitzy mused aloud, once again ignoring everything Lulu had said.

"Dental Floss! Dental Floss!" Bard and Herman called out before returning to building their contraption.

"You guys better not have stuffed him!" Lulu yelled before turning back to Garrison.

The two exchanged a knowing look; they clearly needed a better plan. Mature tactics, such as talking, obviously held very little weight with these boys. Both Lulu and Garrison felt disappointed; they had been hoping for a speedy resolution. Between their own fears and Sylvie, there was more than enough on their plates; adding a kidnapped bird to their agenda felt downright overwhelming. Shuffling gloomily away from the tree, Lulu and Garrison were greeted by Hyacinth, who was dressed in a pink pantsuit with Celery perched stoically on her shoulder.

"Besties! Besties! Have you found Toothpaste yet?"

"Not quite," Lulu responded curtly. "But you are

more than welcome to stay and annoy the Contrarians while we formulate a new plan."

"You got it, bestie. I've totally been wanting to bond with the Contrarians! You know how much I love making new besties," Hyacinth said excitedly, holding up her hand for a high five.

Garrison and Lulu ignored the young girl's hand and headed back toward the Contrary Conservatory. Determined not to waste a perfectly good high five, Hyacinth carefully pushed her hand against Celery's small paw.

"Hey, Fitzy! Bard! Herman! It's me, Hyhy, your new bestie! That's short for 'best friend.' But you guys probably already know that, since it looks like you are a besties trio," Hyacinth babbled as she focused in on the strange contraption they were rigging. "What are you doing with all that rope?"

"We're building a bungee jump," Fitzy called down proudly. "Only we couldn't find any bungee cords, so we're using rope instead. Now that I think of it, I guess that makes it a rope jump, not a bungee jump."

"Rope jump! Yeah!" Bard and Herman seconded from beneath their large brown mops of hair.

"Is that safe?" Hyacinth asked, reviewing their highly

questionable engineering from her position on the ground.

"I don't know," Fitzy replied nonchalantly.

"So how exactly does the whole thing work?"

"We tie the rope to your legs, you jump, and then you bounce. Pretty cool, right?"

"Hold on a second," Hyacinth said, leaning closer to the ferret. "Celery would like to be the first ferret to ever bungee jump. She's been looking for a way into the *Guinness World Records* and she thinks this might be her best shot. It's either bungee jump or try out for *Dancing with the Stars* again. But honestly, bestie to bestie, I don't think *Dancing with the Stars* is going to happen. They're clearly ferretists, maybe even rodentists."

"Wait, so you want your ferret to bungee jump?" Fitzy asked, clearly confused by Hyacinth's ramblings on the anti-rodent position of *Dancing with the Stars.*

"*I* don't want her to do anything. *Celery* wants to do it," Hyacinth carefully clarified.

"Ferret bungee jump!" Bard and Herman screamed in unison.

"Awesome," Fitzy called out, pumping his fist in the air.

"Thanks, Fitzy! I think you're totally awesome, too! I've always wanted a ginger-haired bestie, and now I have one!" Hyacinth said as she shimmied up the tree with Celery on her shoulder.

Once on the branch, Hyacinth began to fret over Celery's safety during the jump.

"This is safe, right? Because Celery is my number one bestie, the bestie of all besties, so she better not get hurt. As a matter of fact, I would be super grateful if you let her borrow a helmet."

"We don't believe in helmets, seat belts, or air bags. They slow down the fun," Fitzy stated definitively.

"Fun!" Bard and Herman grunted loudly, pumping their fists in the air before refocusing their attention on the ropes.

"Fitzy, I wouldn't let Theo hear you talk about safety like that; it's kind of his religion, if you know what I mean," Hyacinth explained. "Now, in light of everything, I am going to have to insist on fastening my hankie into a harness and my watch into a helmet for Celery."

"A ferret harness and helmet? Cool," Fitzy said with a nod.

After creating a harness out of her hankie and wrapping her watch around Celery's head, Hyacinth attached the rope. Planting a quick kiss on the animal's furry cheek, she let go. And while Hyacinth couldn't say for sure, she could have sworn Celery pumped her little ferret fist as she fell.

"Good thing Celery went first; that rope is way too long," Hyacinth said to Fitzy as her ferret landed a mere three inches from the ground. "You would have cracked your head open, maybe even died."

"No way," Fitzy said before a momentary look of concern washed over his flat, pancake-like face. "By the way, Bard thinks Celery is totally cool. If you're into it, he'd like to stuff her when she dies and keep her as a pet."

"That's sort of creepy; I need to rethink being besties with Bard."

A short while later Hyacinth bounded into the Contrary Conservatory's crowded kitchen, eager to share the news of Celery's jump with the other School of Fearians.

Theo, Madeleine, Lulu, and Garrison were in the middle of searching the cupboards for food when the pantsuit-loving girl and her ferret arrived.

"Besties! I have the most amazing news!" Hyacinth squealed as Celery sat with windblown fur on her shoulder.

"You found Toothpaste?" Madeleine asked enthusiastically.

"You found food?" Theo inquired, holding up a carburetor.

Most bizarrely, Basmati did not keep a single particle of food in the kitchen. All the cabinets and even the refrigerator were chock-full of automotive parts, everything from fan belts to transmissions.

"Oops! I totally forgot to ask about the bird. But on the bright side, I have good news about a ferret: Celery bungee jumped! Isn't that amazing? She's the first ferret to ever do it! Talk about a trendsetter!"

"Actually, Hyacinth, I think it's rather inappropriate to allow a ferret to engage in an extreme sport like bungee jumping," Madeleine responded in a most unyielding manner.

"Yeah, I've got to agree with Maddie," Garrison said,

pushing his blond locks from his overly tanned fore-head. "That's pretty uncool, even for you."

Hyacinth's face dropped dramatically as she realized her friends did not approve of her behavior. As she had always loathed the sensation of disappointing others, she immediately deflected all accountability.

"Don't blame me! It was Celery's idea! She begged me to let her do it! I had no choice; she's absolutely desperate to get into the *Guinness World Records.* You have no idea how hard it is to deal with a fame-obsessed ferret," Hyacinth babbled while Madeleine, Lulu, Garrison, and Theo looked on with mounting condemnation.

"Hyacinth, you need a lesson in personal responsibility. *You* agreed to drop your pet ferret, an animal incapable of understanding the ramifications of her actions, off the top of a tree. That's messed up," Lulu said emphatically.

"Lulu's right; your behavior is shameful," Madeleine offered critically as she adjusted her shower cap.

"If I ever hear that you've allowed anything like this to happen again, I'm sending Celery straight to the Pet Protection Program. She'll get a new name, a new owner—an all-around new leash on life," Theo rambled dramatically.

"The Pet Protection Program doesn't exist and you know it," Lulu admonished Theo while rolling her eyes.

"Um, thanks for blowing my cover! What's next? Are you going to report me to the IRS for not declaring my paper route?" Theo retorted with visible annoyance.

"Besties," Hyacinth said softly, "I'm really sorry. You know how important it is to me to be a good friend."

"Sometimes being a good friend is about saying no, about trying to do what's best for your friend regardless of what they say," Madeleine explained seriously.

"Guys, let's get back to what matters: the bird. We have only two days left to find Toothpaste, or School of Fear's over," Garrison proclaimed forcefully. "And since coming out and asking the boys didn't work, we need *another* new plan."

"I say we covertly follow them. Eventually they'll have to check on Toothpaste, at least to give him food and water," Lulu suggested.

"Covert just happens to be my middle name," Theo boasted before pausing to clarify. "Well, technically it's Murray, but you know what I mean."

"You can't even follow yourself covertly, let alone those boys. Maddie and I will handle this; we're the most discreet and the least likely to sing," Lulu said, looking conspicuously at Theo and Hyacinth.

"I don't know; I'm not very keen on being outdoors because of all the spiders and such," Madeleine said meekly.

"Maddie, you slept in the basement last night. There must have been thirty or forty spiders in there alone. If you can handle that, you can handle this," Garrison stated assuredly. "Plus, you wouldn't want me to think you were a pansy, would you?"

"All right, we'll start immediately after lunch," Madeleine acquiesced with a giddy grin.

She'd had no intention of smiling, but in truth, Madeleine simply couldn't stop herself; she was utterly delighted to share an inside joke with Garrison.

CHAPTER 14

EVERYONE'S AFRAID OF SOMETHING:

Diplophobia is the fear

of double vision.

L unch turned out to be a rather perplexing affair, served on a handcrafted Norwegian table dating from the late 1800s. Paper plates and plastic cutlery adorned the grand table, which was stationed smack-dab in the middle of Basmati's Japanese sand garden. Seated in tall-backed, gold-leafed chairs, Mrs. Welling-ton, Schmidty, Abernathy, Basmati, and the School of Fearians waited impatiently for the arrival of the Contrarians.

"You're lucky you don't have any cats," Theo said absentmindedly, looking at the sand. "They'd turn this place into one big bathroom."

"Honestly, Theo, this is hardly an appropriate conversation to have around food," Madeleine said with exasperation.

"I disagree!" Basmati rebuked Madeleine firmly. "We shouldn't hide the painful truth from food. It deserves to know that it will soon be eaten and discarded as waste."

"You want us to discuss what happens to food after we eat it? And during a meal, no less?" Madeleine asked incredulously. "I realize that I'm British and perhaps a smidge stodgier than the rest of you, but you cannot be serious."

"Serious about what?" Basmati asked, lifting his lone eyebrow.

"About discussing bodily functions at the table!" Lulu blurted out.

"How vile!" Basmati responded with a look of total abhorrence. "Honestly, Edith Wellington, I would have expected you, of all people, to impart manners to your students."

"Speaking of manners, where are *your* students? We've been waiting for more than ten minutes," Mrs. Wellington shot back with barely stifled aggravation.

"Wrong!" Basmati snapped. "It's only been nine minutes and thirty-seven seconds, which just happens to be exactly how long I like to wait before starting without them."

Upon hearing this, Theo lobbed half of his sandwich into his mouth. Instantly overwhelmed by the potent taste, he struggled to identify the contents. Never in all his years of extensive eating had he come across this particular flavor combination, which he soon recognized as peanut butter and asparagus on whole-wheat bread.

"You know how you can like both ketchup and ice cream individually, but hate them as a couple?" Theo whispered quietly to Lulu as she took her first bite of the sandwich.

Within half a second, Lulu wholeheartedly understood Theo's analogy. While not as revolting as the offensive-tasting Casu Frazigu, the sandwiches were far from delicious, except to Basmati. He considered asparagus the perfect complement to peanut butter. Then again, he also deemed chocolate the ideal sauce for spaghetti and meatballs.

"Is there any salt?" Theo asked Basmati, desperate to try to improve on the gastronomical aberration.

"Why would you want salt? Are you trying to imply my food is bland? That I'm a bad cook?"

"No, not at all! I've always been a fan of *innovative* cuisines," Theo babbled nervously. "I just happen to like salt."

"I hate salt," Basmati responded venomously, uncomfortably holding Theo's stare.

"Well, I certainly can't deny that salt raises your blood pressure and causes you to retain water," Theo said, patting his stomach.

"I'll let your comments about salt pass this time, but be warned, if you insult pepper, I won't stand for it. I may sit for it, but that's only because I have arthritis in my knees," Basmati admonished Theo before returning to his sandwich.

"I don't know about you, but I am having a great time," Lulu whispered sarcastically to Madeleine. "It's almost as much fun as hanging out with Munchauser."

"Do you think Garrison was right about all those

spiders living in the basement? Is it possible that being outdoors is safer than inside?" Madeleine asked Lulu seriously, clearly preoccupied with the notion of human/creepy-crawly cohabitation.

Lulu began mentally preparing a spider pep talk, which was to center around a single fact: less than one percent of spiders are poisonous. This information, along with a plethora of other useless tidbits, came courtesy of Theo. Lulu often wondered if he moonlighted as an employee for Wikipedia. There was simply no other explanation for his vast knowledge of random facts.

"Heeeelllloooo," a familiar voice wafted faintly through the air.

"Did you hear that?" Theo asked the others as his stomach turned, most likely a result of eating an asparagus-and-peanut butter sandwich.

"Of course! Who could miss the sound of you masticating your food?" Mrs. Wellington snapped. "It's like a cow chewing a hundred pieces of gum at once!"

"Well, excuse me for not having a pair of soundproof dentures, unlike someone I know!"

"Are you implying I wear dentures?"

"Please," Theo said, performing a Lulu-worthy roll of

the eyes, "don't even try to deny it; I can smell the Poligrip from here!"

"I'll find my way in there soon enough," the voice continued breathlessly from beyond the fortress wall, prompting all but Mrs. Wellington to turn their heads with alarm.

"Oh, dear," Schmidty said as he pushed away his asparagus-and-peanut butter sandwich.

"Don't tell me you can smell the Poligrip, too?" Mrs. Wellington huffed.

"Madame, didn't you hear her voice?" Schmidty asked, perplexed that his hearing was superior to the old woman's.

"Whose voice?" Mrs. Wellington asked as Abernathy looked directly at her and snarled.

"Oh, stop acting like such an animal!"

"You're the one who treated me like an animal, making me wear a collar!"

"You were a child, and I was afraid you'd get lost!"

A strange amalgamation of sniffing, grunting, and squealing outside the wall quickly grabbed everyone's attention.

"That pig is worse than a cold sore; absolutely impossible to shake!" Mrs. Wellington snapped as she angrily banged her fist down on her sandwich.

"This place will only make my story all the more likely to win the Snoopulitzer! I'll find a way in there, just you wait and see! I'm not afraid of a little moat or barbed wire!"

Sylvie's comment crawled uncomfortably beneath Basmati's fair skin, irritating the man to his very core. He pulled at his half-mustache aggressively as he stared directly at Mrs. Wellington.

"As is the case with you, privacy is a necessity to do my job well. So it should hardly come as a surprise that I don't take kindly to reporters lurking around my school. You better make sure that woman stays outside the wall, or you'll have more than Abernathy to contend with," Basmati whispered harshly to Mrs. Wellington before standing and skipping back to the house.

It was a most abnormal manner in which to exit considering his sour mood and advanced age, but Basmati wasn't normal.

"I can smell your secrets from here, and soon I'm

going to share them with the whole world," Sylvie called out with the kind of mouthwatering excitement usually reserved for Theo in a bakery.

"She really does have some nose," Lulu said with equal parts disdain and awe.

"I agree. If she was smart she'd work airport security, although I'd hate to see any German shepherds out of a job in this economy," Theo added sincerely.

"How close is the pig? We mustn't let her get over the wall. Our situation is precarious enough," Mrs. Wellington worried aloud.

"By the sound of it, I don't think she's crossed the moat yet," Garrison assessed, his upper lip growing sweaty at the thought of water nearby.

"Why don't we ask the boys if they can see Sylvie? They have a better view than anyone from way up there," Hyacinth said as she pointed to Bard, Herman, and Fitzy, who were standing on the highest point of the Contrary Conservatory's roof.

"What are you doing up there?" Theo howled as he jumped to his feet, alarmed by the boys' proximity to the edge.

"We're going to fly!" Fitzy screamed excitedly.

"People cannot fly! At least not without paying a few hundred dollars to an airline, which, as an aside, doesn't even include checking a bag anymore," Theo yelled in response.

"Don't worry; we built jet packs," Fitzy explained before high-fiving both Bard and Herman.

"I love a good high five," Hyacinth mumbled to Celery as a large rock flew over the fortress wall, landing mere inches from Schmidty.

"Was that an asteroid?" Mrs. Wellington asked seriously.

"No, Madame. It most certainly was not."

"You can't escape me or my story!" Sylvie hollered disturbingly before being drowned out by chanting.

"Jet packs! Jet packs!" Bard and Herman repeated animatedly.

"Wait! Please! Just wait!" Theo screamed at the Contrarians before turning to his lunch mates. "As a hall monitor I cannot sit by and allow this to happen. I have a duty—a duty to safety."

"Theo, I totally support this whole hall-monitor thing,

but the roof is pretty high. I'm worried you'll get vertigo and fall off or something," Garrison answered, pushing his hair out of his face.

"Celery thinks this is a bad idea, seeing as you're super clumsy on the ground; she doesn't even want to know what could happen on the roof," said Hyacinth.

"Don't do it. They can handle this kind of thing; you can't," Lulu added with a frightened expression. "You could really hurt yourself, like, permanently."

"Now I know how soldiers feel heading off to war," Theo said dramatically, dabbing his eyes with his sausage-like fingers.

"Mister Theo, you really don't need to do this—those boys are not your responsibility," Schmidty said genuinely.

"Oh, you'll be fine. Just remember to ask them about the bird," Mrs. Wellington whispered to Theo, completely disregarding the warnings of Schmidty and the others.

"I will do my very best," Theo stated stoically before saluting Mrs. Wellington and marching off.

Theo darted around the side of the Contrary Conservatory, where Bard, Herman, and Fitzy had leaned an extended ladder against the structure. But as the house was so very tall, the ladder didn't quite reach the area of the roof where the boys were standing. This left a large portion of the wall for Theo to scale with neither a harness nor a safety net. If he fell, he would definitely injure himself, perhaps even require a trip to the emergency room. However, as Theo was miles from civilization without access to a phone, reaching a hospital would be nearly impossible.

"What am I doing, risking my life for these hooligans?" Theo muttered, assessing his highly perilous position atop the ladder. "Have I lost my mind?"

As the clammy-handed boy prepared to back down the ladder, he caught a glimpse of his hall-monitor sash, which stopped him dead in his tracks. Theo had to at least try to stop the Contrarians, or he wouldn't be able to live with himself. Or even if he could live with himself, he wouldn't be able to maintain his hall-monitor status. And frankly, Theo wasn't sure life was worth living without a sash.

After pausing to catch his breath, Theo ventured cautiously off the ladder and onto the wall. Although visibly petrified, he was also deeply impressed by his uncharacteristically brave behavior. It certainly wasn't every day that Theo threw precautions by the wayside, but since he had become a hall monitor he could no longer ignore the safety illiterates of the world. He now saw it as his job to educate them, regardless of the danger to himself.

Small ledges of unevenly laid bricks were all Theo had to hold on to as he slowly made his way up the wall. White-knuckled and sweaty-palmed, he maneuvered carefully from one spot to another. The already-perilous scenario disintegrated quickly when the brick beneath Theo's left foot dislodged. Pins and needles pricked his left leg as he grappled to find another step. Hysteria took hold, blurring Theo's vision and incapacitating his muscles. Thoughts of broken bones, internal bleeding, and hospital food passed frantically through his mind. He was spiraling out of control and would soon lose his grip, both literally and figuratively, if he didn't do something. Unable to back down the wall and afraid to climb higher, Theo paused to release a whimper. Only it wasn't a whimper that came out, it was a song.

"If you want my tummy, and you think its yummy, come on girl and let me know," Theo warbled quietly until he found the courage to take his next step.

By the second verse of his highly questionable song, Theo had managed to pull his rotund body safely atop the roof. While the climb had taken only seven minutes, he had sweated out every last drop of moisture in his body, leaving him with dry eyes and a parched mouth.

Highly dehydrated, Theo quickly surveyed the rooftop terrain, a dangerous mishmash of valleys and peaks. Then, meticulously watching his footing, he made his way toward the Contrarians. First in his line of vision was Herman, who stood eerily still, with his toes dangling over the edge. While Theo knew the boy was alive, his physical demeanor offered nothing to support that fact. Bard, on the other hand, was moving about manically, twirling his arms in circles. So continuous was the movement that Theo actually felt a touch of motion sickness just watching him. And finally, sandwiched between the two tall and lanky boys, was a smiling Fitzy. He was clearly thrilled Theo had come for the takeoff.

All three Contrarians sported homemade jet packs constructed out of cardboard, wire hangers, and batteries. Most disturbingly, the jet packs appeared more like a child's science project than an actual technological feat.

For example, all the keys and buttons had been poorly drawn on with markers. Rather astonishingly, despite this, the Contrarians still appeared wholly confident in their contraptions' ability to support them in flight.

"What are you guys doing? You could kill yourselves!" Theo chastised the three dimwits as he slowly approached.

"No way," Fitzy grunted, clearly not believing Theo's dire assessment of the scenario.

"Yes, Fitzy, it's the truth! You guys could die if the jet packs don't work, and I'm pretty sure they won't since you made them!"

"The packs will totally work. Just see for yourself," Fitzy said before turning to Bard and yelling, "Go for it!"

"I'm flying!" Bard called out as he leaped off the roof without so much as a second thought. Of course, he wasn't so much flying as plummeting to the ground. As expected, the red start button, drawn on with a pen, failed to ignite the device. Within seconds Bard boisterously crashed, instantly igniting both terror and guilt in Theo.

"Oh, no! Bard's dead, and I'm an accomplice!" he cried. "I'll never survive jail! I can barely handle the cafeteria! My life's over! And so is Bard's!"

"Relax," Fitzy admonished Theo. "It takes a lot more than that to kill someone, right, Herman?"

Herman nodded his head, marking the first time he had moved since Theo arrived on the roof. The statuesque boy then stepped casually off the edge while pushing his jet pack's red start button. Once again, it failed to work, leaving Herman at the mercy of gravity. A most painful and raucous sound erupted as the boy crashed to the ground seconds later.

"I guess we should have tested the jet packs before we came up here," Fitzy muttered to himself before casually shrugging off the thought.

"You didn't test the jet packs? Why wouldn't you test them while you were safely on the ground?" Theo asked in horrified amazement.

"Test runs, thinking ahead, and all that kind of stuff feels like a waste of time. It's not like anything *really* bad has ever happened to us. Sure, we've broken bones and ruptured organs, but who hasn't?"

"Fitzy, you are in deep, deep denial about the dangers of life! This may actually be the worst case I've ever seen. You need an intervention! Right now!" Theo screamed, wiping his brow. "Life is dangerous. Did you know a woman once died from eating watermelon because the waiter had used the same knife to cut raw meat? A fourteen-year-old boy died after kissing his girlfriend, who had eaten peanut butter two hours earlier; he was allergic! And don't even get me started on the number of people who fall in the bathtub and die all alone, naked and wet! The world is filled with tons of ridiculous, stupid ways to die, and yet you guys feel it's necessary to tempt fate by jumping off a roof with homemade jet packs. I just don't get it."

"I hate it when peanut butter sticks to the roof of my mouth," Fitzy said idiotically before stepping right off the roof. However, unlike Bard and Herman, he didn't even bother to push his red start button.

Theo lunged futilely after Fitzy as the boy's tree trunk–shaped body plunged out of sight. Feeling the need to confirm that all three Contrarians had in fact survived the jump, he inched closer to the edge until Bard, Herman, and Fitzy came into view. Luckily, they had landed atop a cluster of interwoven topiaries, which broke their fall and prevented any serious injuries. Aside from a few bumps and bruises, the boys appeared to be all right, not to mention downright happy. But then again, as they were adrenaline addicts, risking their lives always had a rather positive effect on their mood.

Relieved that the three foolish Contrarians had survived, Theo quickly scanned the fortress perimeter for any signs of pink. Surprisingly, he saw neither sprinkle nor spot of the nosy reporter's luminous skin. Then, after almost a full minute, a terribly obvious fact dawned on Theo. Not only had he forgotten to ask about Toothpaste, he was stuck on top of the roof without even the faintest idea how to get down.

CHAPTER 15

EVERYONE'S AFRAID OF SOMETHING:

Cnidophobia is the fear

of stings.

Marooned on the roof, Theo did what any normal boy would do; he broke into a cheer. With imaginary pom-poms in hand, he began projecting his voice loudly to the garden below: "Give me an H! Give me an E! Give me an L! Give me a P! HELP! I'm stuck on the roof! Help, I'm stuck on the roof! Save Theo! Save Theo!"

A short while later Abernathy rigged an extension to the top of the ladder and aided Theo in his return to the ground.

"It was like I was Rapunzel up there!" Theo said dramatically to Lulu, Madeleine, Garrison, and Hyacinth as he happily stepped off the ladder and onto solid ground. "All I can say is, thank Heavens for Abernathy, aka my platonic prince, or I'd still be up there."

"Okay, now is a good time to stop this whole fairy-tale analogy before it gets too weird," Lulu said, craning her head to watch the Contrarians, who were still splayed out atop the well-sculpted shrubs.

"Celery loves fairy tales! She even dressed up as Rapunzel for Halloween last year. It was impossible to find a wig that fit her small head, so I had no choice but to shave my sister's doll and make my own. But it was all totally worth it when Celery won best ferret costume at the carnival."

"Were there other ferrets at the carnival?" Madeleine asked quizzically.

"Um, hello? It was a ferret carnival!"

"Kansas must be a terribly odd place to live," Madeleine muttered to herself.

"We've got movement," Garrison interrupted as he watched the Contrarians crawl slowly off the topiaries.

"You ready, Maddie?" Lulu asked.

"I don't know; what if we have to hide in a bush or

something while following them? There could be bugs or spiders!"

"Don't worry, Maddie," Theo said bravely. "I'll step in for you!"

"Sorry, Theo, but you make way too much noise to be a spy," Garrison explained before placing his hand on Madeleine's shoulder. "I didn't want to have to tell you this, but I've already seen four spiders inside the house. At least out here there's more space; they can spread out."

Madeleine nodded as Garrison then put his other hand on Lulu's shoulder.

"Remember, girls, don't get too close, and once you know where they're keeping Toothpaste, come back and get us. I don't want you guys going in there alone."

As the two girls nodded their understanding, Theo grabbed Madeleine's arm and said, "If you happen to overhear anything about my heroic attempt to stop them from jumping off the roof, please try to remember it word for word."

"Celery thinks you're super obsessed with yourself," Hyacinth told Theo with her usual peppy grin as Madeleine and Lulu skulked off after the Contrarians.

"Self-obsessed? Ha! I am merely researching a book

that I am writing on myself! A book, I might add, that lots of people are already clamoring to read. Well, maybe not lots of people, but I'm definitely excited to read it, after I write it, that is...."

Hours later, as the sun crept out of the afternoon sky, Basmati surprised Abernathy in the kitchen, dressed in pink swim trunks, a green tie, and a purple jacket, but without a shirt. The look was rather memorable, even for Basmati.

"Abernathy, I've been searching everywhere for you."

"Why?"

"I thought you'd like to stroll through the gardens with me."

"No, thanks," Abernathy muttered meekly.

"So it's true what Edith Wellington says about you...."

"What has she been saying?" Abernathy asked with burgeoning aggression.

"She said you've always preferred to be alone and that you've unfairly used her as a scapegoat for all your life's problems."

"That is not true! If she had left me and my father alone, everything would have been fine! I wouldn't have had to break my promise! I would have had a normal childhood, and maybe even turned into a normal adult!"

"Come, Abernathy," Basmati said with a smile. "Let's discuss this further in the garden."

As the sun faded completely from view, long, warped shadows decorated the ground of the prickly cacti garden.

"Edith Wellington also mentioned that she thought you were the reason your father died so young."

"What?" Abernathy said, fighting the urge to cry. "That's the worst thing she's ever said!"

"Worse than calling you ugly?"

"She called me ugly, too?"

"No, she didn't call you ugly. Actually, she didn't say any of those things. I just made all that up."

"Wait—are you serious? That was all a lie?"

"Yes, but don't be mad. I did it for you. Wasn't it nice to feel justified in your hatred for a few minutes?" Basmati said with a smile.

"I don't even know what to say," Abernathy answered

quietly, still reeling from the ramifications of Basmati's flip-flopping statements.

"You're welcome? Your hair looks good? Really, any compliment will do."

"You're sick."

"I certainly hope so; I was in the Hospital for Spreading Contagious Diseases just this morning. Oh, and by the way, everything I told you was true...."

"So she *did* say those things about me?"

"You seem to care an awful lot about what she thinks of you."

"No, I don't!" Abernathy protested loudly as his body tightened, his temples pounded, and his blood pressure skyrocketed.

As Abernathy attempted to regain his composure, the sound of Sylvie's sniffing once again wafted over the soaring stone wall.

"Hello? Hello? Is someone there? Don't worry, I'm not dangerous. I'm just a traveling saleslady whose car broke down a ways back. I've been wandering the woods for hours looking for something to eat or drink. Won't you let me in? Please!" Sylvie whined faintly from outside the fortress.

"*No hablo ingles*," Basmati replied in pitch-perfect Spanish.

"What did you say?" Sylvie called out.

"I said I don't speak any English!" Basmati hollered as he yanked Abernathy away from the wall and out of the reporter's earshot.

∞

A mere twenty feet away, hidden behind a row of elm trees, was Mrs. Wellington. Dressed in an unfashionable orange pantsuit that precisely matched her eye shadow and lipstick, the old woman was staring directly up at the clouds. While it certainly wasn't obvious, she was praying to the Great Beauty Queen in the Sky. Feeling most desperate and distraught about her situation and her hair, she decided it was time to seek spiritual counsel. Unfortunately, the prayer was brought to an abrupt halt when the Contrarians crawled across her six-inch carrot-colored heels.

"Pardon me, boys, but what exactly are you doing down there? Is this some sort of psychological regression? Are you getting in touch with your inner infants?"

"What?" Fitzy replied with understandable confusion.

"Why are you crawling on the ground?" Mrs. Wellington asked exceptionally slowly, clearly believing the boys to be thick.

"It's really weird, but I can't remember. Maybe we broke our feet? Guys, what are we doing down here?" Fitzy asked the equally perplexed Bard and Herman.

While the Contrarians had escaped the jet-pack disaster without any broken bones, they weren't as lucky where concussions were concerned. After wobbling on their feet and experiencing bouts of extreme nausea, the trio had decided it best to crawl. Alas, short-term memory loss from their concussions erased this fact from their minds.

"If you haven't a clue why you're crawling, might I suggest you rejoin the rest of us humans in standing erect?" Mrs. Wellington bristled.

The Contrarians trembled and swayed as they returned to their feet. While the three boys fought to remain vertical, Mrs. Wellington neither lent a hand nor asked if they were all right. It was a most bizarre way for a teacher to behave, but she wholeheartedly believed the boys needed to suffer the consequences of their foolish actions.

"You look really familiar," Fitzy said, rubbing his temples, desperate to relieve the thunderous pounding.

"Do you subscribe to *Pageant Princesses*? I was the January 1965 cover girl," Mrs. Wellington said proudly.

"*Pageant Princesses*? Is that like *Cat Fancy*?"

"Well, that depends; do the cats wear tiaras?"

"Wait a second!" Fitzy said with a satisfied smile. "You're Larry's grandma!"

"I am no one's grandma!"

"Yeah, right! You look exactly like Larry!"

"Well, seeing as I have no children, it's highly unlikely that I'm Larry's grandma!"

"Man, that's sad—an old lady who isn't someone's grandma. I didn't even know that was possible," Fitzy babbled as Bard and Herman nodded their heads in agreement.

"Sad? There is absolutely nothing sad about being an independent woman without offspring! Nothing at all!" Mrs. Wellington said passionately as her eyes began to well with tears.

"No, I think you're sad," Fitzy declared before Bard and Herman chirped in unison, "Totally sad."

"Fine! I *am* sad!"

"Maybe Larry will let you adopt him so you can have a grandkid."

"I don't want a grandkid! I just want my stepson!" Mrs. Wellington exclaimed emotionally before rushing off in her high-heeled shoes.

As the old woman vanished into the faint evening light, Madeleine and Lulu prepared to inch closer to the Contrarians, having heard a muffled mention of Toothpaste, or at the very least something that sounded like "Toothpaste." The covert spying had been under way for hours, but much to their chagrin had yielded no results. Not only were they trailing erratically behaved boys, they were doing it on their knees. The Contrarians' bizarre decision to crawl everywhere had greatly increased the difficulty of the operation.

While staking out their next plan of action, Madeleine and Lulu heard the unmistakable panting of an English bulldog. Along with flatulence and snoring, heavy breathing is a well-known characteristic of the breed. As Macaroni preferred the company of people, it was hardly a surprise when Theo was discovered next to the dog, shoving crackers into his mouth. Most delighted to have found food — in the washing machine, of all places — Theo was crunching happily away when Lulu popped her head around the hedge.

"What are you doing here?" Lulu whispered with unmistakable annoyance.

"We're your understudies, in case anything goes wrong," Theo mumbled as cracker crumbs tumbled down his doughy chin.

"Theo, spies don't have understudies."

"Then why is there an Understudy Spy Club on Facebook?"

"There isn't; you just made that up."

"Ugh!" Theo grunted, slapping his knee. "You know me too well."

"Now get out of here, before you blow this whole operation."

"I love the sound of that word, 'operation' — well, in this context anyway. Because let's be honest — who likes surgery?"

"Theo, stop talking and go back inside," Lulu whispered through gritted teeth.

"But what if something goes wrong? You may need a chubby bulldog and a mildly overweight man."

"What could we possibly need from you? Sandwiches?"

"Let's leave sandwiches out of this," Theo responded protectively before flinching at the sudden sound of a young girl's bloodcurdling scream.

"Monster!" Madeleine spat at the sight of a millipede and its hundreds of legs. While the prefix suggests otherwise, millipedes do not in fact have a thousand legs, but as far as Madeleine was concerned, anything more than four was too many.

"What could happen?" Theo said, nodding triumphantly at Lulu. "Madeleine could happen, that's what."

"I feel something on my leg!" Madeleine screamed hysterically as she took off running past Lulu and Theo, toward the Contrary Conservatory.

As the sound of Madeleine's small feet pounding against the ground faded, Theo stood up and started stretching, much to Lulu's confusion.

"What are you preparing for, a yoga class?"

"Um, I've been sitting down for almost ten minutes. If I'm not careful I could pull a muscle."

Having had their curiosity piqued by Madeleine's scream, the Contrarians quickly made their way over to Lulu and Theo. There were few things that intrigued them quite as much as shrieking—mostly because they associated it with highly hazardous activities.

"That was so cool! Did you light her shower cap on fire? Burning plastic is my favorite!" Fitzy declared enthusiastically.

"Fire! Fire! Fire!" Bard and Herman chanted disturbingly while tossing Petey the stuffed red snake back and forth.

"Did you know that one hundred twenty-four people in the United States died from snake bites in 2009, and another four hundred four urinated on themselves at the sight of a snake? That's four hundred four ruined pairs of slacks and skirts," Theo said, motioning to Petey.

"Theo," Lulu said with a sigh, "some facts, especially ones concerning bodily functions, are better kept to yourself or, if absolutely necessary, written in your diary."

"I don't have a diary; I have a mournal, aka a *manly* journal, in which I write very *manly* thoughts. Things like 'spend more time at Home Depot' and 'find out where Zac Efron shops,'" Theo proudly explained to Lulu.

"Wait a second, what were we talking about again? It's like my mind just erased itself," Fitzy grunted, rubbing his temples.

"That is so weird; you really don't remember what we were talking about?" Lulu asked, prompting all three Contrarians to shake their heads. "You were telling us where you stashed Toothpaste."

"What's this about toothpaste?" Fitzy asked before pausing, "Oh, you're talking about that bird."

"Please don't tell me you killed him," Theo mumbled before dramatically covering his mouth with his hands.

"No way. I promised my mom I wouldn't kill anything this summer," Fitzy responded casually.

"What have you killed before?" Theo inquired nervously.

"Snails, but it was a total accident. They crawled right in front of my golf cart. But since I'd stolen the cart, I couldn't stop and do mouth-to-mouth."

"This place should be renamed the Convict Conservatory. We're looking at the future criminals of America right here," Theo announced judgmentally to Lulu.

"Thanks," Fitzy said with a nod before he and the other Contrarians wandered off into the night.

"He *would* think that's a compliment," Theo mumbled as he and Lulu made their way back to the Contrary Conservatory.

Upon entering the house, Theo and Lulu discovered the other School of Fearians eavesdropping through the Standing-Room-Only Sitting Room door. Ever the snoops, they immediately joined their classmates, eagerly pressing their ears against the wood.

"Celery wants to know if you could possibly breathe any louder?" Hyacinth whispered as she strained to hear over Theo's bulldog-like panting.

"Well, excuse me for having a deviated septum!"

"Did you get anything out of the Contrarians?" Garrison asked Lulu, totally ignoring both Hyacinth and Theo.

"Does a headache count?" Lulu replied, rolling her eyes. "I know it's hard to believe, but they actually might be dumber than we previously thought and, surprisingly, that's not a good thing."

The sound of Basmati's voice instantly silenced the School of Fearians.

"You are despicable! You hate your own stepson!" Basmati screeched at a near-deafening decibel level.

"That is entirely untrue! I never said any such thing!

Nor did I have an affair with an alien!" Mrs. Wellington replied furiously.

"Oh, stop lying! That alien was the love of your life! It was Abernathy's father you hated!" Basmati countered fiercely.

The impact of such a statement momentarily silenced everyone.

"She would never have said she hated my father. Me, maybe, but never my father," Abernathy said weakly, clearly exhausted by the dueling eccentrics.

"You are my husband's son; I could no more hate you than I could hate him," Mrs. Wellington choked out, her voice overwhelmed with emotion.

"Wow, Basmati knows what he's doing," Lulu whispered with great surprise.

"Does this mean the plan's actually going to work?" Madeleine asked skeptically.

"I think so," Garrison replied optimistically.

"High fives all around!" Hyacinth said excitedly.

And so the group happily slapped hands before making their way downstairs, blissfully unaware what the night had in store for them.

CHAPTER 16

EVERYONE'S AFRAID OF SOMETHING:

Atychiphobia is the fear

of failure.

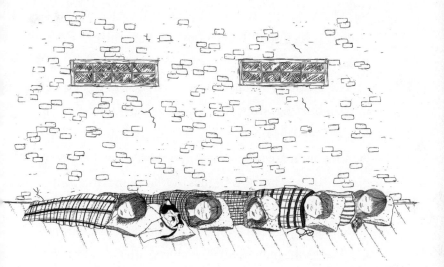

At exactly 2:38 AM a figure shrouded in darkness slipped silently into the Contrary Conservatory's subterranean basement. The silhouette crept cautiously on tiptoes toward the mound of sleeping School of Fearians. Macaroni, sandwiched between Lulu and Garrison, once again proved his complete and utter ineptitude as a watchdog. Not only did he fail to bark, he failed to even wake up as the sinister figure stood watch over the unsuspecting students. Rather shockingly, the first to take notice of the intruder was none other than the ferret. However, due to some unresolved issues over Hyacinth's inaccurate translations of her chirps, Celery decided against waking her owner.

The shadowy stranger cast a large fishing net over the slumbering students and animals. Of course, as Madeleine slept upright, the net settled atop her head, creating an inadvertent tent. In a most disturbing coincidence, this act occurred just as Madeleine dreamed of being ambushed by a gargantuan spider. Caught unceremoniously between a nightmare and a confusing reality, Madeleine panicked. Convinced that a monstrous spider was fast approaching, she decided upon a most unlikely form of self-defense: kung fu. Madeleine had never so much as taken a lesson, but she had once spent an entire night watching Jackie Chan films with her cousin Chester.

"What's happening?" Lulu screamed groggily as Madeleine's arms and legs whipped around inside the tent.

"It's Spidzilla!" Madeleine shrieked as she continued her aggressive assault on the imaginary spider.

"Oh, no, I'm a dolphin trapped in a fishing net!"

Theo moaned, clearly still half asleep. "I need to get back in the water before I die!"

"What water?" Garrison screamed. "Did the pipes burst?"

"We need to get out of here!" Lulu hollered.

"This is the craziest bestie bonding ever," Hyacinth squealed energetically as the chaos continued.

After realizing that the pipes hadn't actually burst, Garrison navigated his way through the sea of arms and legs and out from under the net. Recalling the location of the light switch from memory, he clumsily felt around the wall. Seconds later light burst into the dark room like an atomic explosion. As the children's eyes adjusted, they focused in on the intruder. Standing before them in pink pajamas and a butchered wig was their teacher, Mrs. Wellington.

"Are you going to tell us what's going on, or do I need to start yelling?" Garrison exploded, clearly annoyed by the late-night visit.

Mrs. Wellington's lips turned crimson as she stared intently at Garrison. Feeling terribly ill at ease, the boy removed the net and rejoined his peers on the floor. As the old woman continued to stare at her students, Schmidty shuffled sleepily into the basement.

"My apologies, children. Madame insisted on waking you up with a fishing net. And as usual I haven't the faintest idea as to the logic behind such behavior."

"It's terribly simple, old man; my contestants are acting like a bunch of scared little goldfish, so I decided to treat them as such."

Perched before them with her right knee bent and her left hand on her hip, Mrs. Wellington emitted such raw emotion that the students momentarily looked away. Anger, disappointment, and anxiety appeared to be exploding from each and every inch of the old woman's crinkled skin.

"I have long considered you a special lot, a group of all-stars, a league of students different from the rest. Courageous, intelligent, and loyal, you stood apart. You were ready and willing to battle anything to conquer your fears. And with this in mind, I made a promise to Basmati. But somehow, here I am, standing before you . . . painfully aware that I was mistaken."

"Oh, no!" Madeleine gasped, absolutely heartbroken. "What have we done?"

Madeleine had long prided herself on being a first-rate student, one who never misses an assignment or disappoints a teacher.

"In the short time since we have arrived at the Contrary Conservatory, Basmati has progressed in leaps and bounds with Abernathy, pushing him to the very edge of forgiveness. And you have done nothing but give in to your fears, inadvertently sabotaging the mission. Toothpaste is a talking canary; how hard could it possibly be to find him?" Mrs. Wellington shouted, literally frothing at the mouth.

"Madame, please try to remain calm."

"If you don't find that bird by tomorrow at sundown, Basmati will forever turn Abernathy against me. And he is not a man to be trifled with; he takes his agreements as seriously as I do my makeup. With a few slips of the tongue he could annihilate any future chances with my stepson. And in case you've forgotten, without Abernathy's forgiveness, I lose the school."

"I'm terribly sorry, but I don't understand. Basmati has made tremendous progress with Abernathy, and yet you think he might turn him back against you?" Madeleine asked, clearly confused by the logic of the situation.

"Basmati's an absolute genius at mimicking people's handwriting; he could write up a few horrid letters and destroy all chances of reconciliation with Abernathy within minutes!"

"But is Basmati really that heartless?" Theo inquired. "I thought you guys have known each other for years."

"In the words of Basmati, a deal is a deal is a deal is a deal is a deal is a deal—"

"Yes, Madame," Schmidty interrupted. "I'm quite sure we get the point."

"I understand why you're angry, but honestly, Mrs. Wellington, we've been trying! Today we followed the Contrarians for hours, and not once did they check on Toothpaste. It just doesn't make sense," Lulu said with frustration.

"The contestants I know, or at least the ones I thought I knew, would find a way—they wouldn't just give in to their weaknesses. What happened to my warriors? I thought you were going to save the school, not just for yourselves, but for all the other kids like you," Mrs. Wellington said solemnly before sashaying out of the basement.

The School of Fearians winced at the sound of the

door closing. They actually felt their teacher's disappointment, much like a slap to the face. Ashamed of their own cowardice, all five of them directed their gaze at the floor.

"Children, I think it best for you all to try to get some sleep now. If we are to find Toothpaste and face Sylvie Montgomery tomorrow, we need to be well rested," Schmidty told them. Then, after a few sweet smiles and nods of his head, he prepared to trek back upstairs to the attic.

"Schmidty?" Garrison called out as the old man reached the top of the basement stairs.

"Yes?"

"We're sorry we let you down."

"You haven't let me down at all. I'm only worried you'll let yourselves down. . . ."

The soft sound of Schmidty closing the door behind him heightened the children's profound state of sadness. Since arriving at School of Fear, they had managed to rise to every occasion. Yet this time, they couldn't. This time, they'd failed.

While the others remained shell-shocked by their emotions, Hyacinth's eyes welled with tears. But as she hadn't any tissues, she used Celery's fluffy body to dab at her eyes.

"This whole thing is my fault! If I hadn't told Sylvie about School of Fear, none of this would have happened." Hyacinth wailed, blowing her nose into Celery's fur, much to the animal's displeasure.

"When I sit back and think about it, I guess this whole thing *did* start with you, Hyacinth," Theo acquiesced as he watched Celery try to clean her snot- and tear-soaked body.

"Shame on you! What a dreadful thing to say!" Madeleine scolded Theo.

"What? It's true, isn't it?"

"Yes, Theo, it's true. But you must remember that it's also true that Hyacinth wouldn't have even met Sylvie if you and Garrison hadn't abandoned her at the Pageant for Pooches!"

Garrison closed his eyes as memories of his own poor behavior came rushing back. If he and Theo had stuck with Hyacinth, as they were supposed to, none of this would have happened. As guilt gnawed away at him, he struggled to figure out what was bothering him more — his actions or being called out on them by Madeleine.

"Theo, Madeleine's right. We're just as responsible for this disaster as Hyacinth. Maybe even more so, actually. After all, we're older than she is, and we should have known better," Garrison said, shaking his head remorsefully.

"Not to get technical, but you're older than I am, too, so does that make this..." Theo said before trailing off under Lulu and Madeleine's harsh glares.

"I think Schmidty was right. We have a big day tomorrow; let's try to get some sleep," Garrison said as he laid his head on Macaroni's pillow-like belly.

"Not to go against Schmidty's suggestion, but I don't think we should go to sleep until we have a plan," Theo said, looking enviously at Garrison's head atop the dog's soft tummy.

"It's the middle of the night, and no one is thinking clearly. I say we wait until morning, when we're well rested," Garrison shot back, muffling a yawn.

"But we made today's plans when we were well rested, and they were both total failures."

"Actually," Lulu corrected Theo, "our stakeout wasn't a failure. It totally could have worked if Shower Cap hadn't screamed at the top of her lungs over some millipede. I mean, for all we know they were just about to check on Toothpaste when she blew a gasket."

"Why are you suddenly calling me Shower Cap, Lulu? And I must say I don't take kindly to being scapegoated for the mission's failure!"

"Fine," Lulu relented. "I won't call you Shower Cap anymore, but truthfully, I don't even know why you're wearing one! When have you ever heard of a spider or bug laying eggs in someone's hair? I'll tell you—*never!*"

"How would you know? Are you running a bug-and-spider institute on the side? Are you collecting data about hair invasions? I don't think so! And while I'll admit I don't know anyone personally that it's happened to, I've read at least two accounts on the Internet. So please keep that in mind when you mock my shower cap!"

"You need to take off the shower cap...*now,*" Lulu declared authoritatively.

"Excuse me, Lulu, but you are not my mum. I do not take orders from you. And might I remind you that two boys had to sit on top of you on the plane so you would make it through the takeoff? You're hardly in a position to look down your nose at my shower cap!"

"Lulu *was* acting kind of crazy on the plane," Theo agreed.

"Said the boy who bought parachutes from a homeless man," Lulu retorted harshly.

"Honestly, Theo, I don't know what you were thinking," Garrison said, shaking his head at the plump-faced boy.

"Well, at least I didn't almost let Sylvie in here because I was too scared to walk over a little tiny bridge!" Theo yelled at Garrison.

"Enough!" Lulu shouted. "I didn't mean to start all this! I just meant that Maddie is better than that shower cap. We're all better than the way we've been behaving."

"Thank you, Lulu," Madeleine said quietly, surprised by the sudden shift in the conversation.

"Tomorrow, when we take down Bard, Herman, and Fitzy and finally find this talking canary, let's do it as our best selves. The ones Mrs. Wellington helped us become," Lulu said sincerely.

"Oh, Lulu, I love it when your other personality comes out! She's so inspiring, it's almost better than Randy Pausch's Last Lecture!" Theo said honestly.

"Who's Randy Pausch?" Lulu responded.

"Doesn't anyone watch YouTube anymore?" Theo answered, exasperated.

"Randy Pausch was an incredible man who decided to record his thoughts on life for his children after he learned he was dying. He understood the importance of letting go of fear and living your life to the fullest. And that's exactly what he did, even as he faced a certain and fast-approaching death," Madeleine explained to the group.

"I want to be the best Hyhy I can be! Super Hyhy!" Hyacinth blurted out. "So Celery and I are going upstairs to sleep by ourselves...."

"What?" the group responded in unison.

"Tomorrow, when I wake up, I want to be my best self. And in order for that to happen, I need to know that I can handle being alone, or at least alone with my ferret."

"Hyacinth, Celery," Theo said, gulping emotionally, "I know we haven't always seen eye to eye—and I mean that literally, as you are both much shorter than I am, and also figuratively, as our personalities have frequently clashed. But right now, in this moment, I am so proud of you both. And the fact that I won't have to listen to Celery chirp tonight in her sleep, well, that's just an added bonus."

"Thanks, bestie," Hyacinth said, playfully punching Theo's arm.

"Careful, I bruise easy."

"Oh, sorry, bestie!" Hyacinth said before she leaned in to listen to her ferret. "Oh, and Celery wanted me to tell you that even though your breath is super stinky in the morning, she's going to miss waking up with you."

"That ferret," Theo muttered as Hyacinth and Celery bounded out of the basement. "Always has to get one last dig in."

"Okay, so the plan is we come up with a plan in the morning. And whatever plan we come up with, we do it as our best selves," Garrison confusingly explained to Theo, Lulu, and Madeleine.

"Wait, so what's the plan?" Theo asked, yawning. "Sorry—I sort of spaced out there for a second. I was thinking about my breath. Is it really that bad in the morning? I mean, is it worse than Macaroni's?"

As if sensing something disparaging was being said about him, Macaroni lifted his ears and looked suspiciously at Theo.

"Stop worrying about your halitosis and go to bed," Lulu recommended.

"But what about the plan?"

"For the last time, there is no plan, except to come up with a plan, and then execute it as our best selves," Lulu explained as fatigue lowered her eyelids to half-mast.

"Exactly," Madeleine agreed with a smile before pausing to touch her shower cap. "But seeing as our best selves start in the morning, I think I'll wait until then to remove my cap."

"Hey! You're not sleeping standing up. That's already a major accomplishment," Garrison pointed out sweetly.

And so, in the darkness of the basement, the School of Fearians closed their eyes to prepare for the day ahead. Moments of great failure and great triumph danced through their dreams, bringing with them bouts of both anguish and joy.

Alone a floor above, Hyacinth and Celery curled up next to the overturned sofa in the Standing-Room-Only Sitting Room. Almost immediately a powerful desire to flee washed over Hyacinth. Her legs twitched as she fought the urge to run back to the safe enclave of friendship downstairs. Yet she remained. Somewhere in Hyacinth's mind, she knew she couldn't keep running from her fear. She had to prove to herself once and for all that she could survive being alone. And so she stayed put, with her heart racing and her legs twitching. By the time dawn broke, Hyacinth was both exhausted and extremely proud of herself.

After slipping out to watch the sunrise, Hyacinth ran her small hand over the cold stone of the fortress wall. Lost in her own thoughts, she was startled by a disconcerting but instantly recognizable sound—snorting. In a move that showed great maturity, she immediately covered her mouth with her hand. While she was pretty sure she wouldn't say anything, she thought it best to take every precaution.

"Good morning, little one," Sylvie said gruffly between snorts.

Hyacinth winced at the power of the woman's nose; she had already sniffed her out. She closed her eyes and wondered what to do. Should she stay and listen to what Sylvie had to say? Maybe even try to convince the crazed reporter to drop the story? Or was that too dangerous? Would she accidentally say more than she intended? Perhaps the only safe plan was to scurry back to the house. As Hyacinth labored over the decision, a most remarkable thing occurred: she heard another voice. As it was deep in tone, timbre, and pitch, she quickly deduced it had to be a man. But who could it be? Who else was in on Sylvie's diabolical plan?

CHAPTER 17

EVERYONE'S AFRAID OF SOMETHING:

Gamophobia is the fear

of marriage.

G ood day," Schmidty greeted Basmati as he stomped into the kitchen in a puffy white wedding dress with a train twice the length of his body.

Much like the one worn by Princess Diana on her wedding day, this dress seemed to have a life of its own. The billowing mess of taffeta and crinoline whispered with each step, the fabrics brushing lightly against each other.

"*Good* day? Is it really a *good* day, Schmidty? How

do we know it's not going to be a *bad* day? There are just as many bad days as there are good days, yet people insist on saying *good* day!"

"Very astute point. I stand most corrected. In the future I shall simply greet people with one word: 'day,'" Schmidty replied to the matrimonially clad man.

"Yes, I think that wise. Now then, I'm off for my final lesson with Abernathy, but remember: if your students do not find Toothpaste, I shall convert him back to his stepmother-hating self quicker than you can say 'Where's your other eyebrow?'"

"I'm hopeful that will not come to pass, that we shall reunite you with Toothpaste and save our school at the same time."

"It's not that I wish School of Fear to fail, but a deal is a deal is a deal is a deal is a deal—"

"Yes," Schmidty interrupted. "I'm quite sure I understand."

"*Good day,* Schmidty."

"Good day, sir."

"What did I just tell you about saying that?" Basmati exploded.

"But you just said it yourself."

"I did no such thing!"

"My apologies, sir. I must have hallucinated," Schmidty said with exasperation. "I wouldn't be surprised if my delusions stemmed from a complete lack of food. Your kitchen is chock-full of cylinders but nary a cracker or crumb."

"I shudder to think of how you were raised. Everyone knows food is to be stored in washing machines, water heaters, and radiators. Who in their right mind keeps food in the kitchen?" Basmati said with disbelief as he stormed out of the room.

"Yes, who in their *right* mind indeed," Schmidty muttered to himself as he went in search of the closest radiator.

After gratefully munching on an array of peanut butter and crackers provided by Schmidty, the School of Fearians returned to the basement to formulate yet another plan. The students, seated in a circle with Macaroni in the center, were understandably tense. They had a responsibility to one another and to Mrs. Wellington, but most of all to School of Fear itself. Without such an institution, future generations of neurotic children would go untreated, dooming them to a life of anxiety and worry.

"Gary, what's the plan?" Theo asked, eating rogue crumbs off his shirt.

"I've always hated losing," Garrison said in a surprisingly philosophical tone. "It made me feel really bad about myself, like all the hard work I put in was for nothing. But now I'm beginning to think I was wrong. Failure forces you to focus on what's really important, what matters most to you. And do you know what matters most to me? Showing the world just how strong we've become, letting them know that nothing can stop us, not even our fears."

Madeleine took a deep breath, said a prayer for a spider-and-insect-free future, and removed her plastic shower cap. After weeks of continuously wearing the cap, the girl felt rather naked without it. And while a small part of her longed to put it back on, she didn't. Madeleine was ready for liberation, from both her fear and her unflattering accessory.

"Give it up for M-A-D-D-I-E!" Theo said as he jumped up and began performing some highly questionable Rumpmaster Funk dance moves. "Go Fearians! Go Fearians!"

"School of Fearians are the best, especially when put to the test!" Hyacinth sang off-key as she joined Theo's impromptu dance party.

"Nice moves!" Theo complimented Hyacinth as he simulated riding a carousel, a dance move he felt was ripe to sweep the nation.

"Not to rain on the parade, but we haven't actually rescued Toothpaste yet. As a matter of fact, we haven't even come up with a plan to rescue Toothpaste. So maybe it's better to hold off on all the celebrating until we've done that," Lulu announced sensibly, prompting the others to nod in agreement.

Nestled in the southeast corner of the gardens, behind a cluster of aspen trees, was an intricately carved chartreuse and pink gazebo. While the color scheme was most unbecoming, an abundance of dried flowers and candles masked it well. Long-dead roses, tulips, and hydrangeas overflowed from the rotunda, creating a scene similar to that of a wedding. Unfortunately, weddings always left Abernathy ill at ease, as they stirred up memories of losing his father to Mrs. Wellington. He had long thought of them as similar to funerals: cause for great sorrow and mourning.

Then Basmati arrived in the elaborate white wedding dress, humming "Here Comes the Bride," which did little to assuage Abernathy's anxiety.

"What a glorious day for a wedding! Absolutely perfect," Basmati said merrily as he marched up the steps, his long train trailing behind him.

While perplexed as to who could possibly be getting married, Abernathy remained mum, worried the answer might include an alpaca.

"I love dead flowers—they're just perfect for weddings," Basmati stated, lightly grazing the flowers with his fingertip.

Abernathy nodded politely while studying the detailed beading of Basmati's bodice. It was a most elaborate creation, clearly the work of a very patient and well-sighted artisan.

"It's a beautiful dress, isn't it?"

"Yes, but doesn't the bride usually wear the dress?"

"In civilized society, the groom wears the gown and the bride the suit," Basmati said snottily, quite literally looking down his nose at Abernathy.

The two exceptionally weird men fell into a prolonged silence, during which Basmati stared intently at Abernathy. While the forest dweller loathed the intrusive gaze, he had come to expect such behavior from the half-mustached man.

"As I am sure you've noticed by now," Basmati said, "I am madly in love with your stepmother, Edith Wellington. And today I shall marry her, making me your stepfather."

"I don't want a stepfather," Abernathy exclaimed quickly, his stomach twisting painfully into knots. "It doesn't matter, anyway; she'll never marry you."

"What did you say?"

"I said she'll never marry you."

"Well, I don't think she'll ever marry *you*," Basmati barked back venomously.

"That's fine—I don't want to marry her!" Abernathy replied with scantily masked hostility.

"Oh, of course, how could I forget? You despise poor old Edith Wellington; you would never marry someone you hate."

"I would never marry *her* because she's my *step-mother!*"

"And?" Basmati asked, shrugging his shoulders.

"And she's family.... Family doesn't marry family, at least not where I come from!"

"So you two are *family*?"

Abernathy paused to breathe as his blood pressure skyrocketed, a terribly common occurrence when speaking with Basmati.

"Yes, we're family."

"And that means you definitely don't want to marry her, right?"

"Right."

"Well, if you don't want to marry her, neither do I!"

And with that Basmati marched straight out of the gazebo, his train flying dramatically behind him. Abernathy stood shocked amid the flowers, one word racing through his mind: "family." He had referred to Mrs. Wellington as family, but what did that even mean? Abernathy hadn't been a part of anything resembling a family since he was a child. He closed his eyes, momentarily overwhelmed; a sudden flash of emotion filled his body as he recalled playing with his father as a little boy. Perhaps he did remember what family was after all.

"Let's get down to business. What's our plan to find Toothpaste? It's got to work, and fast, because we still need to convince Sylvie to pull the story," Lulu announced to the School of Fearians, who remained seated in a circle on the basement floor.

"Celery and I think the best way to handle Sylvie is to talk to her friend. She seems super scared of him, like he's her dad or dentist or something, so she'll do whatever he says," Hyacinth remarked offhandedly to the group.

"What are you talking about?" Lulu exploded as Garrison simultaneously exclaimed, "What friend?"

As everyone reacted to her comment, Hyacinth merely shook her head angrily at Celery, who was perched atop her shoulder.

"Oh, no, did Celery forget to tell you? She's become

super unreliable lately; maybe it's Alzheimer's? Or amnesia? Or ferret dementia? Or—"

"Hyacinth!" Lulu snapped with frustration. "Just tell us what happened."

"Okay, so Celery and I decided to watch the sunrise this morning, in honor of our super-duper accomplishment of sleeping alone. Although, in truth, we didn't really sleep at all—"

"Do you think you could tell us what happened *a little faster?*" Lulu interrupted through gritted teeth.

"We were walking next to the wall and we heard Sylvie talking to a man."

"And what makes you think it was her dentist? Were they talking about gingivitis? Plaque? Root canals?" Theo asked seriously.

"Chunk, Hyacinth didn't mean her *actual* dentist, just someone she's afraid of *like* a dentist," Lulu clarified.

"Oh, I see," Theo said with a knowing nod. "I get it—dentists can be scary. I'm actually in hiding from my last one; he made me give up chocolate, soda, ice cream...all sugar-based products. It was like being back at fat camp all over again!"

"I could be wrong, but I'd bet my good name that the

man is the editor of Sylvie's paper. Think about it: Who else would she trust to bring in on such a big story?" Madeleine pondered, biting her lip ever so slightly.

"Good point," Lulu agreed.

"The editor is probably looking to confirm the facts, make sure she isn't another Stephen Glass or Jayson Blair." Madeleine surmised.

"I think I speak for everyone in the room when I say we have no idea who Jayson Blair and Stephen Glass are, or what they have to do with Sylvie," Lulu said, brusquely pushing her strawberry blond locks away from her freckled face.

"They're notorious American reporters who received a great deal of attention for breaking the most unbelievable stories. Only it was later discovered that the articles were fabricated."

"This is exactly why I don't read the paper!" Theo huffed dramatically. "Well, that and because I hate getting ink all over my fingers."

"So you think the man is Sylvie's editor?" Garrison wondered aloud.

"Yes. It's the only plausible explanation I can think of," Madeleine stated confidently. "Unfortunately, it might make dealing with Sylvie a bit harder, as she'll loathe admitting defeat in front of her boss."

"Aren't we getting ahead of ourselves? We still don't have a plan to rescue Toothpaste. And without Toothpaste, we lose the rehabilitated Abernathy, leaving us with nothing to undermine Sylvie's story," Lulu pointed out logically.

"I've got an idea! Let's dress up real tough, like with leather jackets and slicked-back hair, and scare the information out of the Contrarians," Theo offered earnestly.

"They jump off roofs for fun; I don't think leather jackets are going to cut it," Lulu responded.

"Celery wants to know why we don't bribe them, figure out what they want and give it to them in exchange for the bird."

"Darn it! That's actually a good idea," Theo said, abashed. "Outsmarted by a ferret again."

"But what do they want? The only thing they've ever shown interest in is lighting things on fire," Lulu pointed out.

"There must be something else. Everyone has a price— especially boys with limited intelligence," Madeleine said shrewdly.

"That's true; I'd do anything for two éclairs and a glass of milk," stated Theo.

"You'd do anything for a stick of gum," Lulu replied with a smirk.

Theo scoffed before relenting, "I guess it depends on how long it had been since I last ate. Gum is a poor substitute for food, but when you're hungry, you're hungry."

"Instead of guessing what they might like, why don't we simply ask them?" Madeleine suggested sensibly.

"I don't know; the direct approach didn't work last time," Garrison responded.

"Last time we weren't offering anything. The promise of goods is a wholly different situation. These boys are essentially pirates—fearless maniacs holding poor Toothpaste hostage. But, like all pirates, they must want something." Madeleine explained confidently.

"Okay, I'm in. Let's do it," Garrison announced, taking to his feet.

"Wait? You want to do it right now? Aren't we going to practice first? Do a dress rehearsal or something?" Theo warbled nervously.

"Theo, in case you haven't figured it out by now, time

is of the essence. We only have today to save the school," Lulu declared firmly.

"*Here we go to meet the boys, who play with pet canaries as if they're toys, and even though they may be strong, we have the gift of song!*" Hyacinth sang in her usual tone-deaf manner.

"*Thanks, I feel better already, now let's go forth, strong and steady,*" Theo replied happily to Hyacinth's song as the School of Fearians made their way up the basement stairs.

CHAPTER 18

EVERYONE'S AFRAID OF SOMETHING:

Batrachophobia is the fear

of amphibians.

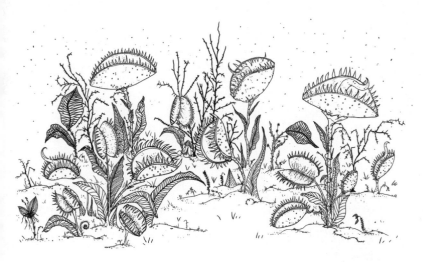

This is like a whole garden of Theos," Hyacinth commented as the fretful Fearians cut through a patch of Venus flytraps, one of the world's few carnivorous plants capable of eating flies and insects.

"Except I'm a vegetarian!" Theo pointed out animatedly.

"I think these just might be the most magical plants in the entire world! They eat insects! Isn't that fabulous?" Madeleine exclaimed delightedly.

"Yeah, I'll be sure to send you a bouquet on your birthday," Lulu replied dryly.

"Actually, Lulu, it would need to be a potted plant, because they won't eat insects unless they're still alive," Madeleine clarified.

"Maddie, I hate to have to break it to you," Theo said, "but Lulu is an imaginary-gift giver. Or, to put it bluntly, she's really cheap and refuses to buy anyone a present."

"Chunk, I thought you of all people would be into imaginary gift giving. I mean, it's way better for the environment. Or maybe you're not as green as you thought?" Lulu said to Theo.

"How dare you? I'm so green...I'm blue and yel-low...as in the colors that make green," Theo retorted awkwardly.

"Wow, that was so bad, it was almost epic," Garrison said as the group came upon a mass of topiaries sculpted into triangles, circles, and squares.

Once they'd made it beyond the well-sculpted hedges, the School of Fearians searched a mini-volcano sur-rounded by lava rocks, a compost garden, and the gazebo, but could find no sign of the Contrarians. Just as they wondered whether it was possible that the boys had slipped back into the house, they stumbled upon a smoldering left shoe.

"If Smokey the Bear had a top ten most-wanted list, these guys would be on it!" Theo said, shaking his head.

"I have to agree; I'm rather surprised they haven't burned the whole place down by now," Madeleine said as Garrison led the group down a path strewn with scorched clothing.

Following the trail of a singed sweater, a burned-out sock, and yet another charred shoe, the School of Fearians finally located the elusive Contrarians. Fitzy, Bard, and Herman, all of whom were noticeably lighter than usual in the clothing department, were using a patch of thick, lustrous ivy as a ladder to scale the wall.

Sensing an opportunity to be a hero, Theo quickly corralled the Fearians into a huddle.

"Seeing as I have been trained in covert tactical operations, also known as hall monitoring, I think it's best if I take the lead. All I need is five minutes and I'll have those boys spilling secrets like most people do milk," Theo announced, brazenly cracking his knuckles.

"Actually, Theo, I think it best for all involved that absolutely anyone but you acts as the mouthpiece for the group. And I mean that in the least offensive manner possible," Madeleine stated honestly.

"You're lucky you have such a nice accent, or that would have really offended me," Theo replied.

"It's not personal; it's just that we need someone the Contrarians can relate to, and frankly, that is not you. Please know that if we were attempting to corral Macaroni, we would definitely enlist your help," Madeleine explained nicely as Hyacinth began to bounce up and down.

"Besties, not to toot my own horn, but the Contrarians totally love me! So what do you say? Can Celery and I do it?"

"Actually, that's not a bad idea," Garrison acquiesced. "They *do* seem to like you—probably something to do with the fact that you let Celery bungee jump."

"Rewarding pet abuse? If PETA revokes my membership, it's on your shoulders," Theo whispered angrily to Garrison.

"I think we should let her do it," Lulu declared boldly.

"Oh my gosh, this is the best day ever!" Hyacinth squealed.

"Well, except for the whole Abernathy/Toothpaste/

Sylvie situation," Theo interjected, clearly irritated that Hyacinth had been chosen as the face of the mission.

"Now, Hyacinth, we need you to try your absolute hardest to find out what the Contrarians want in exchange for Toothpaste. It's very important that you stay focused," Madeleine explained seriously.

"Don't worry, besties—Hyhy and Celery are on the case! Hyhy started this whole thing, and Hyhy is going to do her part to end it."

"She's talking about herself in the third person already? Talk about a power trip," Theo moaned jealously.

Fitzy, Bard, and Herman were halfway up the ivy when the purple pantsuit–clad Hyacinth arrived at the base of the wall.

"Hey up there, besties! Celery and I are super excited to see you guys! We're so excited we may have to sing a song! Do you guys have a harmonica with you, by any chance? Celery is really good on the harmonica; she's kind of a ferret prodigy."

"The bungee-jumping ferret!" Fitzy yelled, fortuitously halting Hyacinth's plan to sing. "We're going moat div-ing! Want to come?"

"Thanks for the invite, but I'm going to have to pass.

But before you jump off the wall and most likely permanently damage your memory, I need to ask you guys a question, bestie to besties."

"Does that mean the ferret's not going to moat dive either?" Fitzy wondered aloud.

"No way! Celery doesn't know how to swim," Hyacinth responded before remembering Madeleine's advice about staying focused. "Okay, so here's the thing: we're prepared to give you anything you want in return for the bird. That means money, food, illegal weapons, contraband, plutonium, knives, a private plane to Mexico…anything."

"How does she expect us to find plutonium? We're not even in high school yet," Theo muttered to Madeleine.

"I wouldn't worry; I don't think they're smart enough to ask for any of it up front."

"So what's it going to be? Knives? Plutonium? Chocolate éclairs?" Hyacinth asked in her most grown-up voice.

"Please say chocolate éclairs," Theo prayed quietly.

"Moat diving!" Fitzy hollered as he dangled precariously off the now strained ivy.

"Wait—you guys will give us Toothpaste if we moat dive?" Hyacinth repeated dubiously.

"Yeah!" Fitzy yelled, prompting both Herman and Bard to follow suit.

"Contrarians, we, the School of Fearians, consider this to be a legally binding, albeit verbal, agreement," Madeleine said litigiously before grabbing hold of the ivy.

"Maddie, what are you doing?" Garrison inquired, his face wet with perspiration.

"I'm doing whatever it takes to save the school. What are you doing?" Madeleine replied pointedly.

"I'll tell you what I'm *not* doing: jumping in a moat!"

"What's the matter? You afraid?" Fitzy laughed uproariously.

"He's afraid! He's afraid! He's afraid!" Bard and Herman chanted, perfectly in sync, before abruptly returning to abject silence.

"Yes, as a matter of fact, he *is* afraid. He is absolutely petrified of jumping into that moat. But so what? We're School of Fearians; it wouldn't make much sense if we weren't afraid of something, now would it?" Theo boldly defended Garrison.

"What's your mascot, the chicken?" Fitzy called out before erupting into a cackle.

"Actually, we don't have an official mascot," said Hyacinth, "but I'd like to take this moment to nominate Celery, who also happens to be the world's first bungee-jumping ferret."

"Excuse me, Hyacinth, but if anyone is going to be our mascot, it's Macaroni," Theo argued. "Not only does he have seniority, he has a much better personality."

"No way! You guys are the chickens! *Bock! Bock! Bock!*" Fitzy taunted as he pulled himself atop the soaring fortress wall.

"*Bock, Bock, Bock,*" Herman and Bard grunted, smirking.

"Don't *bock* at us! We're not *chickens*!" Garrison responded, his competitive nature rising to the surface. After years of playing sports, he had come to view taunts as a warm-up for an excellent game. At that moment, adrenaline rushed through his system, priming him to prove Fitzy and the Contrarians wrong by any means necessary.

The School of Fearians broke into two groups so as not to overstrain the ivy. Garrison and Lulu scaled the vines first, followed by the remaining three. Worried his weight might rip the ivy off the wall, Theo insisted on going last. At least that way, if he fell, he wouldn't crush anyone.

The top of the wall was dreadfully narrow, leaving barely enough space for the children's feet. And while the Fearians swayed with nerves, the Contrarians remained the epitome of calm, cool, and collected. Of course, after years of hazardous behavior they were desensitized to danger.

In a desperate bid to ignore the bubbling mass of water beneath him, Garrison counted the treetops on the skyline. However, even with his eyes averted there was no avoiding the moat's noxious odor, an unpleasant reminder of the water's proximity. Without any viable means of escaping the impending jump, Garrison forced himself to confront the monster at his feet. A strange and powerful disconnect took hold, separating Garrison's mind from his body. The world appeared to be a movie, something he was watching from a distance. He didn't care that barbed wire crawled dangerously along the wall's exterior, because he wasn't actually there.

Minutes passed as Garrison stared calmly at the

bubbling water below. Then, in an abrupt shift, his body and mind realigned, bringing reality into sharp focus. This was not a movie. Garrison was watching his own life. There was no escaping the fact that he was the boy standing atop the wall, preparing for the enemy to swallow him whole.

"This is going to be so cool!" Fitzy screamed, electrified by the idea of moat diving.

"Hyacinth, I realize you were put in charge of this mission, but I'm going to have to step in on this one," Theo explained authoritatively before turning toward the Contrarians. "As the resident safety expert, or 'safepert' for short, I would like to inform you that hitting the water from fifty feet or higher is equivalent to landing on concrete."

"How high is this wall?" Fitzy asked with sudden interest.

"I estimate twenty, twenty-five feet."

"Are you positive?" Fitzy pressed on. "Because landing on concrete really sucks; that's how I broke my leg last summer."

"How high up were you?"

"Only three or four feet, but we were going about twenty miles an hour."

"Please tell me you didn't jump out of a moving vehicle," Theo said with sudden concern.

"Is a motorcycle a moving vehicle?"

"Something tells me Fitzy is not going to do well on the SATs," Lulu mumbled snidely under her breath.

"Why would you jump off a motorcycle? Was it on fire? Were you about to drive off a cliff?" Theo asked suspiciously.

"My uncle was taking me for a spin on his bike when I suddenly remembered it was my grandpa's birthday. And he gets really mad if you forget his birthday, so I jumped off the bike to go call him."

"That is a disturbing story on many, many levels," Theo replied matter-of-factly, shooting his fellow School of Fearians a concerned look.

"But Fitzy, surely you've done this moat dive before?" Madeleine asked in a most professorial tone.

"Nope."

"I see," Madeleine said, nodding her head. "But you've checked the depth of the moat?"

"Nope."

"Fitzy, you do realize that if the moat is too shallow, you could wind up paralyzed and unable to move your arms or legs? You'll be in a wheelchair for the rest of your life," Madeleine cautioned.

"Unless, of course, there are advances in stem-cell research," Theo corrected her.

"Theo, now is not the time for scientific sidebars," Lulu interjected.

"Wait a minute—you're saying I could be in a wheelchair for the rest of my life?" Fitzy repeated with palpable concern.

"Yes, that is *exactly* what I am saying. Thank you for *finally* listening," Madeleine replied gratefully.

"No way! You're making that up!"

"No, Fitzy," Madeleine reassured him, "I most certainly am not."

"But I risk my life all the time, and nothing ever happens...."

"Well, you've been extraordinarily lucky, but at some point everyone's luck runs out. You do understand that, don't you?"

"Are you saying my luck could stop *right now,* like with *this jump?*" Fitzy asked, shocked.

"Anytime you do something reckless, like jumping into a moat, you run the risk of sustaining extreme bodily harm that could permanently stop you from leading an active life," Madeleine stated emphatically.

"Then I'm not jumping!" Fitzy screamed with uncharacteristic panic, clearly petrified by the idea of being immobile.

"Me either," Herman and Bard seconded, agreeing with Fitzy, as they always did.

"Have you guys *really* never considered the possibility of grave bodily harm before?" Madeleine asked in amazement, to which the Contrarians shook their heads.

"I just never thought that it was possible to have too much fun, so much fun that you can't ever have fun again," Fitzy explained, scratching his head. "I'm still pretty young; I can't spend the next fifty years sitting down...no way! I haven't even climbed Everest yet!"

"This feels like the perfect moment to impart a few Theoisms to you," Theo said. "Number one: don't skimp on the mayonnaise; it's a pivotal part of building the perfect sandwich. Number two: the world isn't a playground, so you need to get the facts before you decide to do something. Number three: if you are feeling sad, eat a fried potato product and your mood will improve—french fries, hash browns, home fries, Tater Tots...any of them will do."

"While I can't speak to the mayonnaise or potato platitudes," said Madeleine, "Theo is certainly correct about getting the facts before doing something bonkers like jumping into a moat. Now, it just so happens that I have the facts in this case. The moat is twenty feet deep, and contrary to what Mrs. Wellington claimed, absolutely piranha free. There's nothing more dangerous than a few warm-blooded salamanders in there."

"How do you know all this?" Lulu asked suspiciously.

"Schmidty mentioned an underwater scuba expedition that occurred last time they visited; something to do with a missing diamond earring," Madeleine said as she grabbed Garrison's left arm and signaled for Lulu to take his right.

"Wait! I'm not ready!" Garrison exclaimed with an excessively pale face.

"You can do this," Lulu stated confidently, squeezing his clammy hand.

"No, Lulu, I can't...." Garrison trailed off, ashamed of his own weakness.

"Come on, don't you want to show me your doggy paddle?" Lulu jested in an effort to lighten the mood.

"I'm not ready...it's all happening too fast."

"Garrison, I believe in you. I always have," Madeleine said sweetly before planting a peck on the boy's tanned cheek. "But trust me: none of this is happening too fast."

The kiss electrified Garrison, drowning him in adrenaline and excitement. In fact, so distracted was the boy that he didn't even notice when he became airborne. Madeleine and Lulu had rather deftly brought Garrison off the wall with them. But now, as he hurtled toward the murky water, his exhilaration morphed into panic.

CHAPTER 19

EVERYONE'S AFRAID OF SOMETHING:

Cleptophobia is the fear

of stealing.

I guess that means we're going together!" Hyacinth said cheerfully as she grabbed Theo's pudgy white hand. "By the way, if we get married, I really want to go to Niagara Falls on our honeymoon!"

"Way to make it awkward! I haven't even asked you to marry me yet. Wait! I didn't mean *yet,* I meant...oh, forget it. Let's just jump already."

In an uncharacteristically responsible move, Hyacinth had left Celery safely on the ground with Macaroni.

After Celery's bungee jump, she felt it best that the ferret avoid all extreme sports, at least until she got her motion sickness under control.

Meanwhile, the warm, bubbly water enveloped Garrison as his body fell weightlessly away from the world. Separated from Madeleine and Lulu, he saw nothing more than a haze of white. A powerful confusion took hold, jumbling the very foundation of his brain. He could no longer tell which way was up. How long had he been in the water? Was he even still alive?

Frightened, Garrison tried to scream, causing his mouth to fill with copious amounts of water. As the boy began to choke, four soft hands grabbed hold of him and pulled him to the surface. Once he was safely out of the water, Garrison immediately started coughing, expelling large quantities of liquid.

"You're fine," Lulu said with a smile as she and Madeleine helped Garrison back to dry land.

"Actually, I'd say you're more than fine—you're fantastic!" Madeleine declared sweetly, prompting Garrison to look away, overwhelmed by the sentiment.

"My skin hurts," Theo warbled as he broke the

water's surface with a grimace. "That was worse than a belly flop; it was a body flop! Even my earlobes hurt."

"That's weird; I feel fine," Hyacinth said cheerfully.

"Listen, about this whole marriage thing," Theo said to Hyacinth. "I know I'm a catch; I mean, I get it. I'm good-looking, kind, and a hall monitor to boot; who wouldn't want to marry me? But sadly, I just can't commit to anyone—not right now, anyway."

"Relax, I was joking," Hyacinth replied. "I would never marry you. Well, at least not as long as Celery's alive. She would have an absolute fit; she might even try to assassinate you. Oh my gosh, I could totally see Celery dropping arsenic in your food!"

"What is wrong with you? Why do you sound so cheery when talking about my demise at the paws of that darn ferret?" Theo huffed as he swam toward the moat's edge.

As Theo and Hyacinth pulled their wet bodies ashore, Garrison, who had finally caught his breath, managed to crack a smile. From Madeleine's kiss to the near drowning, he had never experienced a rush of adrenaline quite like that in his life.

Fitzy, Bard, and Herman still stood atop the wall,

looking down at the group. Even after watching the School of Fearians survive the jump without sustaining serious bodily harm, the Contrarians still appeared greatly rattled by the idea of moat diving. Fitzy's pasty, freckled legs shivered as he contemplated being immobile for life. Now that the idea had been firmly planted in his head by Madeleine, he was incapable of shaking it. But at the same time, he had no intention of stopping the fun, as that would be worse than death. And so, after Fitzy gave a quick nod to Bard and Herman, the three Contrarians jumped off the wall. However, there was a notable difference in the boys' demeanor as they fell: none of them made catcalls or pumped their fists in the air.

After they'd jumped and then emerged from the moat, the eight soggy and unbelievably stinky children lounged on the banks, allowing the sun to wash over them. For the Fearians, this was a well-earned respite on the road to recovering Toothpaste. Having already completed their end of the deal, they were momentarily excused from all responsibility. But the relief was short-lived: suddenly the sound of a man shouting jolted the Contrarians and Fearians alike.

"No!" the man screamed, his voice echoing through the trees, obscuring the origin of the sound.

"Yes!" Sylvie Montgomery hollered emotionally in response, her voice also reverberating greatly.

"That sounds like my grandparents. Do you think they followed me? They can travel pretty fast with their walkers," Fitzy asked genuinely.

"I can pretty much guarantee that those aren't your grandparents," Garrison stated confidently.

"Are they *your* grandparents?"

"No, my grandparents are dead," Garrison answered bluntly.

"That would make it even cooler: zombie grandpa!"

"Guys, unless you want Sylvie and her friend to join your little conversation about zombies, I think we better get back inside the fortress," Lulu said patronizingly, shaking her head at the boys.

"Not to nitpick, Lulu, but how are we going to get in? The drawbridge is up," Theo said perceptively.

"No worries—we'll just dig a tunnel!" Fitzy announced excitedly with a fist pump.

"Yeah!" Bard and Herman seconded before following Fitzy a few feet away to begin digging a tunnel…*with their hands.*

"I think we can all agree that the Contrarians' plan is

fanciful at best," Madeleine determined, watching the boys dig most incompetently. "So, back to Theo's surprisingly astute question: How are we going to get in?"

"Maddie, why are you so surprised that I asked a good question? I have tons of good questions! For example, just off the top of my head, why isn't there any good Mexican food in New York City? Do airlines really wash the blankets after each flight? Why isn't Washington, D.C., a state?"

"Theo, there is a lot to be said for quitting while you're ahead. Consider that the first of many Luluisms I will be imparting to you between now and the start of high school," Lulu said with a smirk.

"No! No! No!" The man again screamed, his voice violently bouncing off the trees.

"Quick, let's go inside; I don't want to come face-to-face with Sylvie again," Hyacinth whimpered. "I don't trust myself around that lady; her nose can get anything out of me!"

"What? You don't think the tunneling is going to work?" Lulu asked sarcastically, looking over at the Contrarians, who were a mere two inches into their project.

"I've got it!" Theo said in his most macho voice before cracking his knuckles. "Schmidty, lower the draw-bridge! We're stuck outside!"

"Why did you need to crack your knuckles before screaming?" Garrison asked Theo.

"Gary, Gary, Gary," Theo said, then paused. "I have absolutely no idea."

"Mister Theo?" Schmidty called out from inside the fortress. "Mister Theo? Was that you?"

"Yes! I need a sandwich, stat!"

"Priorities!" Garrison chastised the endlessly hungry boy.

"I meant, lower the drawbridge, and *then* make me a sandwich!"

"Doesn't anyone else think it's odd that Sylvie has yet to appear? After all, she's been stalking us for days, and we just heard her talking to someone, and yet, she still hasn't presented herself. Something's not right," Madeleine observed.

"Yeah, why hasn't Sylvie come running after us? She's desperate to get a quote for the story," Lulu concurred.

"Would everyone please stop talking about her?"

Hyacinth pleaded. "I'm feeling super nervous, like I might start yelling secrets...just exploding information!"

"Honestly, Hyacinth, you're worse than WikiLeaks!"

"Is that some sort of boring British cartoon?" Hyacinth asked Madeleine sincerely.

"WikiLeaks is an organization that publishes loads of top secret documents—just plunks them out there without any thought of consequences, kind of like you!"

"Schmidty?" Theo called out. "How's that sandwich...I mean drawbridge coming?"

"Maybe it's not a big deal that we haven't seen Sylvie. She could be off somewhere, licking her wounds after the row with the editor," Madeleine surmised unconvincingly as the soft creaks of the rickety wooden drawbridge filled the air.

"I tried licking a wound once; what a mistake that was! Blood tastes terrible; it gave me a whole new respect for vampires," Theo muttered.

Five feet away Fitzy, Bard, and Herman continued their exercise in futility, also known as digging a tunnel with their hands.

"Come on, guys, let's go," Lulu called out to the Contrarians as the drawbridge slammed loudly into place.

"Wait!" Fitzy responded eagerly. "We found a buried treasure!"

"Gold!" Bard and Herman screamed simultaneously.

"Never mind, it's just a hard clump of dirt," Fitzy said with visible disappointment. "Guess I'm going to have to wait and get rich the old-fashioned way."

"Don't worry, Fitzy; hard work is underrated," Madeleine offered with a smile.

"Who said anything about hard work? I was talking about lottery tickets."

"Of course you were," Madeleine replied wryly as the Contrarians started across the bridge.

While the Fearians were most relieved to have Toothpaste in their sights, they couldn't shake their concern over Sylvie's absence. She was a most tenacious snoop and would never forgo an opportunity to interview the children without a great reason. But what was the reason? And, more to the point, how damaging would it prove to School of Fear?

CHAPTER 20

EVERYONE'S AFRAID OF SOMETHING:

Necrophobia is the fear

of dead things.

Toothpaste

"Contestants! Contestants! Where is the bird?" Mrs. Wellington cried. "Have you any idea how antsy that half-mustached man is? He's following me around the house threatening to shave my left eyebrow! I'm already bald, with a botched wig! I can't lose an eyebrow!"

"Calm down, Mrs. Wellington," Lulu said. "We're going to deal with it right now. The bird will be in our hands in five minutes."

"Five minutes, Lulu, five minutes," Mrs. Wellington repeated gravely. "If I spend the rest of my life drawing on an eyebrow, that's on your shoulders."

Already burdened by the weight of the mission, Lulu now had to worry about Mrs. Wellington's eyebrow as well. In truth, if the old woman weren't already so weird-looking, Lulu would hardly care. But the loss of an eyebrow just might push her into the freak category.

The School of Fearians found the Contrarians using the hose as a substitute shower. Still wearing their clothes, Bard, Herman, and Fitzy took turns spraying one another with the ice-cold water.

"Hey, guys, do you know how to turn the hot water on?" Fitzy asked.

"It's a hose; there is no hot water," Garrison replied.

"Oh," Fitzy replied with genuine surprise. "I thought this was the shower."

"I'm frightened to ask what he thinks the toilet is," Theo mumbled under his breath.

"We need Toothpaste, now," Lulu stated firmly as thoughts of a one-browed Wellington flashed through her mind.

"Ah, Toothpaste," Fitzy said, breaking into a mischievous smile. "Can we talk about him later?"

"No way," Lulu replied. "We want the bird now."

"Later…"

"Boys, need I remind you that we have a legally binding verbal agreement, which explicitly states that you are to hand over Toothpaste after the completion of our moat dive?" Madeleine asked in her most litigious tone of voice.

"You're still going to have to wait," Fitzy responded nonchalantly.

"Excuse me?" Lulu said, brimming with indignation. "You guys might be crazy, but trust me, we are way crazier! You do *not* want to mess with us! Now give us back the bird!"

"We can't," Fitzy answered quietly.

"I knew you were dumb and really bad dressers, but I never would have guessed you were liars," Theo said with unmistakable disgust.

"This behavior is absolutely abominable, even for people of your great intellectual shortcomings!" Madeleine huffed angrily.

"You guys are such…such…" Lulu yelled heatedly as she searched her mind for the right word, "jerks!"

"She called us jerks," Fitzy babbled proudly to Bard and Herman, who then both repeated, "Jerks! Jerks!"

"Do you even realize what you're doing to us? To our school?" Garrison asked the Contrarians as Hyacinth whispered into Celery's ear.

As Garrison continued his verbal attack on the Contrarians, the furry little animal ran down Hyacinth's body, across the ground, and straight up Bard's leg. Then, with the skill of a covert spy who also happens to be a rodent, Celery grabbed Petey with her mouth and removed him from Bard's pocket. So deft was Celery's theft that she was halfway back to Hyacinth before Bard even realized what had happened. And by the time his brain told his body to go after Petey, the stuffed snake was firmly in Hyacinth's hands.

"Petey!" Bard yelled emotionally, staring at the taxidermied reptile held tightly in Hyacinth's grasp.

Relishing her newly acquired sense of power, Hyacinth smiled mischievously. There was a great deal of pleasure to be had in tormenting the Contrarians.

"First things first: you are no longer my besties; effective immediately, that title has been revoked," Hyacinth announced seriously. "Now, on to your snake."

"Please don't hurt him!"

"Um, Bard? Petey's already dead," Theo reminded him. "What could she possibly do to him?"

Madeleine elbowed Theo, warning him to stop his inadvertent weakening of Hyacinth's position. A threat to the well-being of the snake was all they had to offer, so ignoring his deceased status was absolutely necessary.

"If you ever want to see Petey again, you need to give us the bird," Hyacinth declared ferociously.

"I am really starting to like you," Lulu said with a strange mix of pride and astonishment over the young girl's bold behavior.

"Oh my gosh! Lulu and I are super besties!" Hyacinth squealed with delight as she broke into a celebratory dance.

"Maybe now isn't the best time to dance over our friendship, seeing as you're in the middle of blackmailing the Contrarians...."

"Petey!" Bard wailed, releasing an animalistic scream.

"How can you do this to your friend?" Garrison asked Fitzy with visible disgust. "What kind of a person are you?"

Fitzy looked at Bard's tormented expression and grunted loudly. Unsure what to do, he bit his lip and closed his eyes. Oddly, the boy remained in this state for nearly thirty seconds.

"Is he meditating?" Theo whispered to Madeleine. "I wouldn't have guessed he was the metaphysical type."

"I believe this is something commonly referred to as stalling," Madeleine answered.

"Oh, come on already! Just spit it out!" Lulu snapped, forcing Fitzy to open his eyes.

"We don't have Toothpaste," he finally said.

"Did you eat him?" Theo asked before covering his mouth dramatically with his hand.

"No! What kind of crazies do you take us for?" Fitzy replied, clearly offended by the insinuation.

"Big ones," Theo replied earnestly. "Big, crazy, mentally imbalanced lunatics."

"So, the thing is, we kind of don't have a clue where Toothpaste is," Fitzy said softly, wincing in anticipation of their response.

"*You kind of don't have a clue where Toothpaste is? What does that even mean?*" Garrison asked suspiciously.

"We don't know where the bird is...at all...."

"What kind of incompetent birdnappers lose the bird? It's deplorable how bad you lot are!" Madeleine huffed angrily. "If you're going to be criminals, the least you could do is be good ones!"

"I have half a mind to report you to the Better Business Bureau! This kind of shoddy criminal activity will not be tolerated!" Theo hollered nonsensically.

"You guys don't understand; we never planned on kidnapping Toothpaste. It was an accident," Fitzy mumbled, his moon-shaped face now cherry red. "We were trying to fly with these cool wings we built, and we wanted to see how a bird flapped up close. So we brought him into the yard to do a few laps, only he flew away immediately. And that was the last we saw of Toothpaste."

"This is just a wild guess, but the wings didn't work, did they?" Lulu commented dryly.

"It ended pretty much like the jet packs, only with feathers," Fitzy admitted.

As the rest of the group fell silent, Bard's whimpering grew more and more pathetic, until finally Hyacinth could take it no more. Desperate to alleviate the boy's pain, she returned her now worthless bargaining chip.

"I really hope Toothpaste isn't agoraphobic," Theo said with sudden concern for the canary's mental health.

"A bird that's afraid of open spaces? I don't think so," Lulu countered.

"Animals have phobias, too! Some of them even have psychiatrists!"

"To be honest, Toothpaste looked kind of relieved to escape. I mean, Basmati did shave the bird's right eyebrow off," Fitzy said, playing with his messy red hair.

"But birds don't even have eyebrows," Madeleine responded, proudly recalling the ornithology section of her biology class.

"All I can tell you is that the bird has a big bald spot above his right eye," Fitzy told her.

"Petey," Bard whimpered, happily hugging his stuffed red snake.

"That's sweet; he seems like a really good dead-pet owner," Theo said matter-of-factly.

"There's just one thing I don't understand: If you never had Toothpaste, why does Basmati think you're holding him hostage?" Lulu inquired intelligently.

"We may not be birdnappers, but we're not dumb—"

"That is highly debatable," Theo interrupted under his breath.

"We realized Basmati would leave us alone if he thought we had Toothpaste. You guys have to understand, he's really weird. After he caught us lighting our shoes on fire, he tried to marry us off to an alpaca."

"All three of you to *one* alpaca?" Theo muttered, "Talk about crowded."

"Contestants!" Mrs. Wellington shouted hysterically from the house. "Contestants! We haven't much time! This man is going bananas! Where is the bird?"

"Abernathy!" Basmati cried out boldly. "Bring me Abernathy!"

"Schmidty, hide him!" Mrs. Wellington hollered frantically. "Contestants, hurry!"

As the hysterical voices of Mrs. Wellington, Basmati, Schmidty, and Abernathy carried on, the Fearians looked to one another, unsure of their next step. Sensing an opportunity to escape, the Contrarians slinked off. Knowing that Basmati would soon be looking for them, the trio went in search of a foolproof hiding spot.

"What are we going to do?" Garrison asked, his mouth suddenly parched from fear.

"If someone can find a picture of Toothpaste, some nontoxic paint, and another bird about his size, I think I can handle this," Theo said hysterically.

"Get a grip! That will never work!" Lulu scolded Theo.

"Abernathy! Come here!" Basmati's voice reverberated through the yard.

"Well, we can't just stand here! We have to do something! Think!" Madeleine panicked as tears welled in her eyes.

CHAPTER 21

EVERYONE'S AFRAID OF SOMETHING:

Arsonphobia is the fear

of fire.

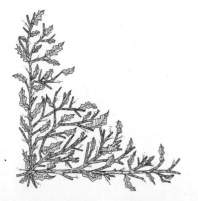

Chaos, like fire, spreads at an alarmingly fast rate. Having realized that Mrs. Wellington was unable to produce Toothpaste, Basmati flew into a hysterical rage. The man screamed, threatened the life of the old woman's left eyebrow, and demanded to speak to Abernathy. Believing that Mrs. Wellington had reneged on their deal, Basmati was determined to stop her from reaping the rewards of his hard work.

Under Schmidty's diligent guidance, Abernathy had

retreated to the topiary garden and was hiding discreetly beneath a well-sculpted hedge. Nearby, Mrs. Wellington desperately attempted to reason with Basmati as he exited the Contrary Conservatory in search of her stepson.

"Please, Basmati! You can't do this to me!" Mrs. Wellington pleaded with the crazy-eyed man. "You must leave Abernathy alone! He's already been through so much!"

"You tricked me—you never had any intention of finding Toothpaste!"

"No! How can you even think that? Why would I do such a thing?"

"Because you've always been jealous of me!"

"Of you? Have you looked in the mirror recently? It looks like a lawn mower rolled over half your face!"

"Abernathy! Where are you? I must speak to you immediately!" Basmati bellowed as the School of Fearians created a human barricade in front of the contrary man.

"Why don't you forget about Toothpaste? I can teach Celery to disagree with everything you say," Hyacinth offered perkily.

"Yeah," Theo agreed, "you can even dress her up as a bird and keep her in a cage!"

At this, Hyacinth and Celery, who was seated atop her shoulder, exchanged worried glances.

"Basmati, you need to believe us; we did everything to find Toothpaste. But the Contrarians don't have him. They never did," Garrison explained.

"I won't listen to your excuses! Abernathy!" Basmati screamed as the School of Fearians continued to block his path.

"Well, well, well," a gruff and gravelly voice declared triumphantly from behind the battling group. "Look who I found!"

The sight of Sylvie Montgomery's shimmering pink skin, much like neon Pepto-Bismol, shocked the group nearly as much as did her presence inside the wall. The nosy reporter tended to grow rather fluorescent when excited, and having finally found her way into the Contrary Conservatory, she was downright elated.

"What did I tell you about letting reporters in, Edith Wellington?" Basmati snapped viciously, still encircled by the School of Fearians.

"How did you get in here, Sylvie?" Mrs. Wellington

queried with palpable horror. "I do not believe that you were able to lug that ample derriere of yours over the wall!"

"The drawbridge is still up," Lulu whispered to Mrs. Wellington after straining to see the entrance to the gardens.

"I didn't know pigs knew how to burrow!" Mrs. Wellington said with contempt.

"Are you implying that I am a pig?" Sylvie barked as she grunted and groaned, sniffing the air.

"Implying? No. I am *stating* that you're a pig."

"Something tells me you won't be so bold tomorrow, when my article runs. Now, seeing as I'm about to tell the world your deepest, darkest secrets, I thought I'd offer you each the opportunity to go on the record, to tell me your side of things."

"I'm sorry to interrupt, especially when you are so *generously* offering to let us explain the secrets you are planning to share with the world," Lulu said sarcastically, "but I really need to know: How did you get in here?" ·

"There's a trapdoor in the northwest wall," Sylvie

grumbled as she continued to draw deep and noisy breaths in through her snout.

"But how did you know about it?" Theo blurted out, proudly displaying his hall-monitor sash to the reporter.

"I have my sources," Sylvie said with a self-satisfied grin.

"Celery says that smirk of yours is really starting to annoy her," Hyacinth said with an uncharacteristic frown.

"Well, Celery certainly isn't the only one," Madeleine huffed, glaring at Sylvie's luminescent pink face.

"Madeleine Masterson, why don't we start with you? Would you care to comment before the whole world finds out you have a major crush on Garrison Feldman? And before you ask, yes, my paper's published in the United Kingdom, too."

Mortification, as Madeleine suddenly learned, is not merely a mental condition but a physical one as well. Nanoseconds after hearing Sylvie's vitriolic words, the sensation of hot water scalding her skin spread across her body. Her vital organs retracted in shame and her eyes welled with painfully salty tears. Madeleine was aware that the others knew of her feelings, but having them publicly declared was simply too much for the sensitive young girl. What if Garrison did not feel the same way? An inevitable wedge of awkwardness would separate the two, ultimately killing their friendship.

As Madeleine looked down at her small navy shoes, both Theo and Lulu put their arms around her in a show of support. Garrison, who was now the color of beetroot, appeared almost paralyzed with fear. He wasn't sure exactly what to say, or to whom. But when he heard the soft sound of Madeleine crying, his instincts kicked in.

"So what's news about Madeleine having a crush on me? I have a crush ... on her ... too," Garrison announced nervously.

"No!" Sylvie snapped. "You have a crush on Ashley Minnelli. I read it in your file myself!"

"I *did* have a crush on Ashley, as in *past tense.* Get your facts straight."

"What file?" Lulu asked, stepping toward Sylvie.

"I'm the reporter here! I'll ask the questions," Sylvie yelled in response.

"I don't think so," Lulu said assuredly. "You may succeed in embarrassing us and ruining Mrs. Wellington's career, but you won't intimidate us; we won't allow it."

"Are you talking about our FBI files? Because I have long suspected I was on their radar, ever since I took part in that renewable-energy rally," Theo said sincerely to Sylvie.

"You *really* think the Feds care about your secrets? You think they're interested in the Covert Eaters Club?" Sylvie shot back caustically.

"How do you know about that? I'm the only member," Theo muttered as a nearby bush rustled lightly. Having ignored Schmidty's quiet pleas to stay firmly hidden behind the topiary, Abernathy had crawled almost twenty feet so he could clandestinely watch what was happening.

"The Covert Eaters Club is just the tip of the embarrassing iceberg," Sylvie announced, smacking her lips and inhaling deeply through her snout. "Remember when you wore a ski mask to your grandpa's funeral because you were afraid death was contagious? Your family was humiliated, especially your beloved grandmother."

"If Chubby's family was even a little embarrassed,

which I highly doubt, who cares? Theo was merely expressing his grief in a unique and original way. He loves his family very intensely, so it should hardly be a surprise that he would also mourn them very intensely," Mrs. Wellington shot back defensively.

"Well, what about Lulu's little bout of appendicitis?" Sylvie asked, turning her eyes toward the strawberry blond girl.

"Please don't publish that story! I'll never get a job; I may even be arrested!" Lulu pleaded frantically.

"Sylvie, you cannot be so heartless! Lulu is but a child!" Mrs. Wellington roared.

"She didn't seem like a child when she broke into Providence General Hospital and stole an appendix!"

"I really needed that appendix!" Lulu wailed. "My teacher didn't believe I had appendicitis; she thought I was just making it up to avoid the trip to the courthouse and those awful elevators! And of course she was right, so I broke into Providence General and took an appendix. But it's not like anyone was using it. The thing was on a bookshelf in some old dude's office!"

"Honestly, Sylvie, you of all people must understand that sometimes we all need to bend the rules a little,"

Mrs. Wellington said through gritted teeth. "But that doesn't mean Lulu should be branded a criminal for life because of it!"

"You all sure do enjoy bending the truth—like when Garrison hid under the house with all those spiders and snakes just to fool his parents into thinking he was at swim practice," Sylvie stated, staring at the tanned boy.

"You really are a vicious and most unsympathetic woman," Mrs. Wellington responded. "He was attempting to make his parents happy, to relieve them of their worry. Plus, what child hasn't fibbed about where he's spending his time? I specifically remember telling my own dear mother that I was off to school when I was really going to the beauty salon. And at the end of the day, getting my hair curled was an education, so it hardly mattered."

"That's where you're wrong; all of this matters—to me, to my readers, and, most important, to the Snoopulitzer committee."

Mrs. Wellington was shaken upon seeing Sylvie's ironclad determination and immediately softened her tone.

"These children came to me for help," she said.

"Please do not punish them for that. You may write anything you like about me, even my real age, but leave the School of Fearians and Abernathy out of it," Mrs. Wellington begged emotionally.

"Speaking of Abernathy, I must find that man; there's something very important I need to tell him," Basmati said cryptically as he pushed past the children and took off into the gardens.

"Abernathy is here? Now I'm definitely winning the Snoopulitzer!" Sylvie grunted eagerly as she waddled after the half-bald man.

CHAPTER 22

EVERYONE'S AFRAID OF SOMETHING:

Neophobia is the fear

of anything new.

Abernathy, you must listen to me: Edith killed your father! I'll show you the letter she wrote confessing to everything!" Basmati yelled as he raced through the gardens with Sylvie, Mrs. Wellington, and the School of Fearians hot on his tail.

With Basmati fast approaching the cacti cluster, Abernathy panicked and attempted to hide behind a tall, lanky cactus. Seconds later, upon entering the garden, Basmati found his eyes immediately drawn to the swathes of plaid and pastel sticking out from behind a lean plant. The emotionally volatile man yanked Abernathy away from the cactus while proclaiming that his stepmother murdered his father.

"Listen to me, Abernathy! Edith Wellington killed your father!"

"Who killed his father?" Sylvie asked, panting, utterly exhausted from chasing Basmati.

"No one!" Mrs. Wellington barked as she closed in on Sylvie in the cacti garden. "It's not true!"

"I have the letter to prove it! And Sylvie, if you leave out any mention of me or my institution, I will be more than willing to supply you with a copy," Basmati screeched desperately.

"How could you?" Mrs. Wellington gasped.

"It's not personal, it's business," Basmati responded coldly.

"So Edith Wellington not only ruined your life, forcing you to live in the forest, but she killed your father," Sylvie said to Abernathy. "Would you care to make a statement?"

As Abernathy pondered the situation, he watched

Theo, Hyacinth, Lulu, Garrison, and Madeleine huddle protectively around the old woman. They knew exactly who she was, and they still loved her. Lulu, unsentimental to the core, sweetly placed Mrs. Wellington's well-manicured but deeply wrinkled hand in hers. Madeleine wiped away tears with her trembling white fingers, only to have Hyacinth offer Celery as a hanky. Surprisingly, Theo did not cry, but instead stood boldly in front of Mrs. Wellington, acting as a human shield. Impressed by his chubby classmate's stance, Garrison joined Theo in protecting their teacher from Basmati's words.

Abernathy continued to gaze at Lulu, Theo, Hyacinth, Garrison, and Madeleine. These were his first real friends, outside of insects and squirrels. He trusted them; he knew them to be flawed but honest people. They believed in Mrs. Wellington, and that was something Abernathy simply couldn't ignore, regardless of how hard he tried.

"Are you that reporter who's going to run the story on School of Fear?" Abernathy asked quietly.

"Yes. I'm Sylvie Montgomery, the future winner of this year's Snoopulitzer."

"Well, then I guess we should talk."

"No!" the School of Fearians screamed. "Don't do this! You're wrong! Please give her a chance!"

Just as Abernathy prepared to open his mouth, Basmati started screaming. And for once, it wasn't about Toothpaste or Mrs. Wellington.

"Fire! Fire!" Basmati hollered as black smoke billowed out of the roof of the Contrary Conservatory.

Basmati, Mrs. Wellington, Schmidty, Abernathy, and the School of Fearians took off toward the house as Sylvie smiled euphorically.

"This just may be the best day of my life! First, an exposé on a secret society, and now a fire... It just doesn't get any better than this!" Sylvie said with delight before waddling after the others.

The top floor of the Contrary Conservatory was aflame, with clouds of heavy smoke pouring from the windows. Fortunately, standing on the ground, covered in soot, were the three Contrarians.

"Someone call the fire department!" Theo screamed.

"There's no phone here, Mister Theo!" Schmidty explained as he frantically searched for the hose.

"I must find the switch!" Basmati shrieked as he dangerously approached the front door of the Contrary Conservatory.

"You mustn't go in there!" Mrs. Wellington hollered. "Step back, Basmati!"

"The switch! The switch!" Basmati repeated as he pulled a red lever on the corner of the front stoop.

Almost immediately, the sound of a complex sprinkler system went off inside the house. As the fire sizzled and smoke continued to pour out of the blackened structure, Basmati turned toward the singed Contrarians.

"Was Toothpaste in there?" Basmati asked with tears in his eyes.

"No," Fitzy replied quietly. "We don't know where he is, but he isn't in the house."

After releasing an audible sigh, Basmati stepped closer to Fitzy, Bard, and Herman, whose hair was unflatteringly charred from the fire.

"In twenty-five years of teaching difficult students,

no one has ever managed to burn down half my house," Basmati said, seething with rage. "Do you have any idea how long it took me to build this place?"

"We're really sorry," Fitzy muttered, as Bard and Herman both echoed, "Sorry."

"We were hiding in the greenhouse, and we wanted to see if burning roses would make the air smell like perfume. And before we knew it, flames were whipping all around us. It was really scary," Fitzy babbled as his burned tee shirt crumbled to dust. "We're giving up danger for good."

"You're giving up danger for good?" Basmati repeated with surprise.

"Yeah," Fitzy grunted meekly. "We're done. We can't take it anymore."

"All of you?" Basmati asked.

All three boys nodded feebly, still reeling from the fire.

"Well, normally I would say you had graduated, but seeing as I still think you know where Toothpaste is, I can't do that," Basmati said coldly.

"I swear we have no idea where that bird is!" Fitzy declared.

"Bird?" Sylvie said quietly to herself.

"I don't believe you! Where is Toothpaste? Toooooth-paaaaaste!" Basmati shrieked emotionally.

"Hello?" a man's deep voice cut through the air.

As everyone looked around, Sylvie sheepishly closed her coat.

"Hello? Toothpaste wants a cracker. Toothpaste wants a cracker. And a car. Toothpaste wants a car, preferably a BMW," the deep voice continued as the group focused in on a highly suspect lump in Sylvie's coat.

"About that source you mentioned—you know, the one who told you about the secret door. It wasn't by chance a little birdie, was it?" Lulu asked knowingly.

"You have Toothpaste!" Basmati exclaimed angrily.

"I have no idea what you're talking about!" Sylvie shot back defensively.

"I love you, Toothpaste!" Basmati screamed.

"I hate you, Basmati," Toothpaste responded from inside Sylvie's coat.

Basmati twirled his half-mustache before letting out an evil cackle that lasted almost thirty seconds. After which he grabbed the pink-skinned reporter by the arms.

"I've always enjoyed the taste of bacon. And you know what bacon is made of, don't you? Dead pig," Basmati said eerily as he opened Sylvie's blue jacket and pulled out a small but terribly animated canary. Just as Fitzy had said, the bird was indeed sporting a bald spot above his right eye.

"Look, I didn't kidnap the bird—he found me! Or he found my sandwich, actually," Sylvie explained. "And then he just started talking and talking. I tried to interrogate him, but it was impossible to have a conversation because he disagreed with everything I said!"

"Good bird," Basmati said, kissing Toothpaste's bald spot.

"Bad human," Toothpaste chirped.

"But then I caught on to his game, and that's how I found the trapdoor. He told me some other stuff, too; my story on the Contrary Conservatory should make an amazing follow-up to the one on School of Fear. Now, then, Abernathy: How about that quote?"

"What quote?"

"About your stepmother," Sylvie said victoriously as Schmidty, Mrs. Wellington, and the School of Fearians grabbed one another's hands in preparation for what was to come.

"Edith Wellington married my father when I was pretty young, and I admit that at first I really didn't like her...not one bit. You see, I had promised my mother I would protect my father, and that is exactly what I intended to do: protect him from all the other women out there. But then I realized maybe that wasn't *exactly* what she meant...."

Mrs. Wellington smiled at Abernathy, tears welling in her eyes.

"Yeah, but when did she send you to the forest?" Sylvie asked aggressively.

"Never."

"What do you mean, 'never'?"

"I mean she never sent me to the forest; I've been at Summerstone this whole time," Abernathy lied.

"I've been training him, preparing him to continue the family legacy," Mrs. Wellington added, tears streaming down her overly made-up face.

"Boring! Who is going to give me the Snoopulitzer for that?" Sylvie snapped before looking at Hyacinth.

"Thanks a lot for wasting my time! No one cares about happy stories; they want misery, drama, destruction! Oh, forget it; I guess I'll just write about Basmati now!"

"How exciting!" Basmati responded joyfully. "Who is he?"

"You are he!"

"I am who?" Basmati answered.

"You are Basmati! And I am writing an article on you and the Contrary Conservatory."

"How could you be writing an article about yourself?"

"I'm not! I'm writing it about you, Basmati!"

"But I'm not Basmati, you are," Basmati shot back emphatically. "And I can have two government officials and a psychiatrist here in an hour to prove it. And then it's off to the sanitarium for you."

"Well," Sylvie blustered, "maybe I should look into that gambling-obsessed attorney instead."

"If I may inquire, Sylvie," Schmidty asked calmly, "was it Munchauser who sold you the children's files?"

"Twenty-five dollars and some inside information on the horses goes a long way with that guy," Sylvie grunted angrily before waddling away.

"You did it, contestants!" Mrs. Wellington said, engulfing the five students in a group hug. "You saved the school! You saved me!"

"We also saved ourselves from total humiliation. I don't know what I would have done if the truth about my girdle came out," Theo admitted.

"Come, children, let's get out of here," Mrs. Wellington said as she led them away from Basmati and the soot-covered Contrarians. "We have a graduation to plan."

"We graduated?" Madeleine said elatedly.

"With honors."

"Does that mean no more summers at School of Fear?" Garrison asked with a tinge of sadness.

"No, not as students—but maybe as counselors," Mrs. Wellington said with a wink.

"Counselor Theo. I like the sound of that!" Theo announced.

"Of course you do!" Lulu, Garrison, Madeleine, and Hyacinth chimed in unison before breaking into laughter.

CHAPTER 23

EVERYONE'S AFRAID OF SOMETHING:

Ecophobia is the fear

of home.

Never in all my many years of teaching have I had the pleasure of meeting five such remarkable individuals. Your compassion and bravery have inspired me, changing the very fabric and quality of my life," Mrs. Wellington announced from behind a silver podium atop a sparkly pink stage on the front lawn of Summerstone.

In honor of School of Fear's graduation, Schmidty had laid out ten rows of silver chairs, a pathway of rose petals, and a large pink stage. The audience, filled with the students' parents and siblings, emanated relief, excitement, and a healthy dose of shock. This was a moment they had long imagined, the day their children's lives were no longer guided by fear, but by their dreams.

Seated on the stage behind Mrs. Wellington were Abernathy, Schmidty, Macaroni, the cats, the sheriff, and Munchauser, all adorned in long silver gowns with matching caps. Directly in front of them, in the first row of the audience, was the graduating class, also dressed in shimmering silver gowns and caps.

"As you go out into the world, life will challenge you. There will be days when fear sneaks back into your mind. But when this happens, remember that I am always here, standing behind you. But more important, your classmates are standing next to you, bolstering you when you are weak and congratulating you when you are strong," Mrs. Wellington said, shooting Schmidty a quick look, prompting the old man to waddle over with the basket of purple, lavender-scented diplomas.

"To avoid even the slightest insinuation of favoritism, I shall call the contestants' names in alphabetical order," Mrs. Wellington announced before pulling the first diploma from the basket. "Theodore Bartholomew."

As his classmates and family cheered, Theo walked proudly onto the stage, stopping to shake the hands and paws of the entire School of Fear team, even Munchauser's. Mrs. Wellington was far too forgiving to simply dismiss Munchauser; instead, she'd demoted him from lawyer to housekeeper.

Standing before Mrs. Wellington at the silver podium, Theo flashed his Vaseline-coated smile to the crowd before performing the traditional pageant wave.

"In light of your great accomplishment," Mrs. Wellington stated while handing Theo the rolled lavender diploma, "I am erecting a Bartholomew family mausoleum at the Morristown cemetery so that even in death, you can always be with your family."

Theo grabbed Mrs. Wellington, hugged her tightly, and mumbled, "This is the weirdest, most morbid gift I have ever received, and I love it!"

Theo exited the stage as Mrs. Wellington looked down at her list and called the next name.

"Garrison Feldman," the old woman called as the audience clapped wildly. Once he, too, had shaken the hands and paws of all seated onstage, Garrison also gave a Vaseline-covered smile and a pageant wave. "In light of your tremendous achievement, I award you a month's worth of surfing lessons with fellow alumnus and surfing great Laird Hamilton."

"You rock, Mrs. Wellington!" Garrison replied before giving the old woman a quick hug.

"Hyacinth Hicklebee-Riyatulle," said Mrs. Wellington, moving the ceremony along, "in light of your remarkable achievement, I present to you a piano, to be stored in a private room at the recreation center so you always have someplace to go and enjoy being alone."

"You really are a super bestie! Like, the best bestie ever!" Hyacinth said as she and Celery, who was squatting atop her shoulder, exited the stage.

"Madeleine Masterson, in honor of your stupendous accomplishment, I give you the rare turquoise spider," Mrs. Wellington said, pulling out a miniature gilded cage from beneath the podium. Inside, a small and incredibly furry turquoise spider slept atop a leopard-print pillow. "Outside of English bulldogs, turquoise spiders are believed to be the most loving and loyal of pets."

"I shall treasure my new friend, although I shall do it from a distance of a few feet, thank you," Madeleine said sweetly before walking offstage.

"Lucy 'Lulu' Punchalower, to celebrate your outstanding and impressive achievement, I present you with a month's worth of private flying lessons in the *Adobe Hornet,* the world's smallest plane."

After a quick Vaseline smile and a pageant wave, Lulu bumped Mrs. Wellington's fist, winked, and returned to her seat.

"This isn't the end of the journey, but rather just the beginning," Mrs. Wellington said, wiping away tears.

Amid cheers and thunderous applause, the five School of Fearians threw their caps in the air and huddled together for an impromptu group hug. They would always have one another, bonded forever by School of Fear and the journey of a lifetime.